RELAY PUBLISHING EDITION, FEBRUARY 2022
Copyright © 2022 Relay Publishing Ltd.

Katie Knight is a pen name created by Relay Publishing for co-
authored Romance projects. Relay Publishing works with incredible
teams of writers and editors to collaboratively create the very best
stories for our readers.

Cover design by Mayhem Cover Creations.

www.relaypub.com

SEAL'S
Surprise Daughter

LESLIE NORTH PRESENTS
KATIE KNIGHT

BLURB

GABRIEL

I'm a father?

One crazy night, and my world is turned upside down.

But I've never backed down from responsibility. Never backed down from *anything*.

Good thing—the woman looking after my daughter is fierce. A momma bear ready to protect her charge, at any cost.

My kind of woman.

CHARLOTTE

My best friend is dead—murdered.

I need to protect her adorable daughter, but I can't do it alone.

I call the only contact number she left for the father, and he picks up.

Gabriel Kelly. Navy SEAL. Gruff. Guarded. Protector. I feel safer already.

It's not just his broad chest and towering size. I know he'll do whatever it takes to keep us protected.

He calls us his family. And I believe it.

I see how his ice-cold exterior thaws whenever his daughter smiles.

And the way he looks at me?

Panty.

Melting.

Falling for our guardian angel was never part of my plan…

But I'm not sure I have a choice.

CONTENTS

ONE

Where the hell is she?

I took another tub of dirty dishes back to the kitchen and dropped them off to my dishwasher, Mel, with a loud clang. Owning the tavern didn't mean I was above working there, too, when needed. Then I jogged to my office to grab my purse, worry gnawing at my insides like a rabid badger. Sure, Alexis could be flaky, especially when it came to getting to work on time, but in the ten months I'd known her, she'd never been late to pick up her daughter from the sitter. Not once.

Of course, Alexis never missed work, either, but she'd totally blown off her shift today. My gut did that sick, twisty thing again. Three hours now, and Alexis still hadn't returned my calls or answered my texts. I handled the orders and tidied the bar, taking on the tasks that Alexis would've done if she'd shown up.

It was that weird time of day between happy hour and dinnertime when things were slower, thank God, but I still had other things I could've been doing. Like inventory or paying the bills to keep the lights on. Or figuring out whether I wanted to sell Rhodes Tavern to some out-of-town franchisors who'd made me an offer.

I pushed thoughts about the future out of my head as I raced out the back door to my car. I needed to get to the sitter's house. Since she couldn't reach Alexis, she'd been calling *me* for the past hour. I sort of liked the fact that I was number two on the phone chain, despite the stress about why I'd been asked to step up.

I couldn't help but smile when I pictured sweet little Savannah. She was seriously the most adorable baby I'd ever seen—and this was coming from someone who wasn't sure they ever wanted kids of their own.

But Savannah looked just like her mama—curly black hair, big green eyes, infectious smile. Except for the ears. They were big for her size and had a little crease at the top that made them distinctive. I assumed Savannah got those from her dad, though Alexis had never mentioned who that was.

She'd come to Harpers Ferry alone and four months pregnant. She didn't like to talk about her past, so I didn't ask. If anyone understood avoiding what was behind you, it was me.

I punched the gas as the light turned green, trying not to worry. Maybe this was nothing more than Alexis needing a break. It was tough being a single mom. I'd watched my own mother go through that growing up, so I knew how much work it was.

Except whenever I'd talked to Alexis the past couple of days, she seemed jumpier than usual. So much so that I'd offered to watch Savannah for her, if she needed, so she could have some time to herself to relax. She'd never gotten back to me on that.

By the time I got to the sitter's house, the sun had set. It was only six thirty, but as fall dragged on the days got shorter and shorter around here. I rushed through the handoff with the sitter, since poor Savannah seemed cranky and overtired. Once I got the baby and her supplies loaded into my car, I headed for Alexis's house.

She was renting a place on the edge of town. Nice. Safe. A one-story ranch that had been converted into a duplex. Alexis had the right side of the place. The other half was vacant at the moment. As I drove, I glanced in the rearview mirror at Savannah dozing in the car seat in the back, finally lulled by the rhythm of the car. Savannah would be six months next week, and she was trying to sit up now.

Alexis was getting her started on baby food, interspersed with formula, since she'd never been able to breastfeed. I smiled and shook my head as I thought about Savannah's feeding schedule. I'd never been so much as a babysitter back in the day, but thanks to her, I'd recently learned a lot about raising little ones.

I made the final turn onto Alexis's street and spotted an explosion of color up ahead, the kind you never want to see. My throat went dry, and my pulse pounded in my ears. This was not good. Not at all.

There were a bunch of squad cars, red and blue lights blazing, in front of the duplex. An ambulance too. I swallowed hard against the bile rising inside me and parked at the curb a few feet behind one of the police cars. Time warped, slow and too fast at the same time. Should I get out?

Yeah, I needed to get out. Find out what was wrong, even though I didn't want to know. I had a horrible feeling that I already did. Something awful had happened to Alexis. I felt it in my bones.

I unclipped my seatbelt, the noise too loud in the quiet vehicle, and Savannah stirred in her car seat. No. If this was going to be as bad as I imagined, I wanted the baby to sleep through it. I wanted to keep her safe, to protect her from whatever was going on here for as long as possible. Thankfully, she fell back to sleep.

Breathe.

My hands were shaking so badly I couldn't open the car door at first. Then, once I finally got it open, an officer was there, telling me I had to move, I had to leave, no one was being allowed into the crime scene.

Crime scene.

Oh God.

"But I'm a friend. Of Alexis Barnes. Sh-she works for me at Rhodes Tavern. I have her daughter in the back seat," I said, my words tumbling over each other. "I-I've been trying to reach her for hours." I looked at the duplex, the front door gaping while cops swarmed the front yard. Figures were silhouetted by the gauzy front curtains, and I had to hold on to the car to keep from collapsing. My chest ached as I whispered, "She never showed up for work today."

"Ma'am," the officer said, looking concerned, his face ashen in the gathering twilight. "You might want to sit down." He paused to glance at the action, then turned his attention back to me. "I'm, uh, I'm sorry for your loss."

"Loss?" My knees gave out. Luckily the car door was still open, and my butt hit the driver's seat instead of the pavement. Just then a stretcher was wheeled out the front door, a white sheet covering the body atop it, and that's when I knew. Alexis was gone.

I remembered from my CPR training at the tavern that when someone was going to pass out, you put their head between their legs and told them to breathe, so that's what I did. Eyes watering, vision tunneling, stomach churning like I was going to vomit any second. Through the roar of anxiety and grief and shock, I heard the officer telling me again how sorry he was.

"What happened?" I managed to get out.

The officer sighed and crouched next to me, his hand on my shoulder. "I'm not at liberty to discuss the case at this time." He glanced into the back seat, then at me again. "Maybe you and the baby could come to the station with me. We'll need you to make a statement."

A statement?

Right. Right. Okay. Yeah. I'd watched enough cop shows on TV to know the routine, even if all this still felt like an out-of-body experience. I nodded, and the cop stood, saying something into his radio before looking back at me. "Do you want to ride downtown with me?"

Transitioning Savannah from my car to his would be a production and probably wake her up. Driving when I was this upset wasn't ideal, but it was better than sitting in the front seat of a patrol car crying my eyes out. "No. I can follow you."

"Okay," he said, walking back to his squad car.

I got back in and closed the door, moving on autopilot. *How is this real?*

In the back seat, Savannah was still sleeping, unaware her mommy was gone. Oh God. Sadness threatened to choke me once more, but I staved it off. I couldn't fall apart. Not yet. I needed to keep it together, for her.

As I waited for the cop to turn around, I grabbed my phone and scrolled furiously through my notes, hands trembling worse than ever, until I reached the one titled "Savannah—Emergency Contact." Darkness settled heavy as a shroud around me as I stared at it.

Alexis had given me the name with an embarrassed laugh, saying that she was being paranoid and ridiculous, but there'd been real fear behind her lighthearted facade—I'd seen it. Why hadn't I pushed her to open up to me?

5

Tears stung my eyes, but I blinked them away fast.

Jesus.

How the hell do you tell someone you haven't seen in ten years that he might be the father of a six-month-old baby he never knew existed?

A train whistle blew in the distance. Eerie and lonesome, piercing the late afternoon like shrapnel.

I'd been standing on this platform for a long time. Too long. Shit. The people there must've thought I was an idiot, missing first one train, then two. Now, the last one to Harpers Ferry was on the way and I needed to be on it.

I paced back and forth in front of the security guard, who was looking more nervous each time I passed. I had a good foot on him, maybe more, and he was probably worried about my behavior. Hell, *I'd* be on alert if I was watching me. I tried to convince myself that I wanted to do this. It wasn't working out so well.

My SEAL team had insisted I return to my hometown on the anniversary of my family's deaths. To make peace with it, they said. For closure. Whatever. I'd made my peace a decade ago when I'd enlisted, and I'd never looked back since.

Fuck it. I was going back to DC. I grabbed my duffel bag and had made it as far as the exit when my cell phone buzzed in my pocket. I pulled it out, expecting to see one of my teammates' names on the screen. I planned to make up some excuse for not going home, then maybe hit a bar tonight, let loose, have some fun. It was my leave time. Why not?

Instead, though, my screen showed a number I didn't recognize, with a Harpers Ferry area code. Confused and intrigued, I answered, against my better judgment. If it was spam, I'd just hang up. "Hello?"

A woman on the other end of the line started talking, her words rushed together like she was in a hurry—or a panic. I'd seen people lose their composure on the battlefield plenty of times and knew the difference. This sounded like the latter. Frowning, I stepped away from the exit so as not to block the way, then concentrated on what the woman was saying.

"This is Charlotte Rhodes. Do you remember me?"

Charlotte Rhodes. The name sounded familiar. It had been a long time ago, but I ran through the people I'd gone to school with, and yep. There she was. Tall, brown hair, pretty. We hadn't been best friends, but we'd hung around with the same group of people growing up. My gut tightened. Why was she calling now? Quite a coincidence. Except I didn't believe in coincidence. "Uh, hey. Yeah, I remember you. What's going on?"

Normally, a call like this might make a person think something had happened to a family member, but I didn't have any. So yeah. I knew it wasn't that kind of call.

"I've become friends with a woman you knew," Charlotte continued. "Alexis Barnes."

I racked my brain again. Alexis Barnes. That name took longer. I finally remembered a woman I'd hooked up with in DC the last night I'd been back on leave, over a year ago. She'd been sweet. Had a bad, stalker-ish situation going on with her ex or something. I remembered a lot of calls and texts coming in while we'd been trying to get to know each other better at the bar. "Sure. I remember her. What's up?"

"She's dead."

Oh. That knocked me back a step. Literally. My back hit the wall, and my duffel hit the floor at the same time. It wasn't that I'd known her that well or anything, but the shock of it. You'd think I'd be used to it by now, but nope.

"She gave me this number to contact if anything bad ever happened to her," Charlotte said, a definite wobble in her tone now, like she was trying not to cry.

"Okay." I raked a hand through my buzz-cut hair and scowled at the floor. This made no sense at all. We'd hooked up one time. We barely knew each other, other than in the biblical sense. We'd spent less than forty-eight hours together. I shook my head and said the first thing that popped into my head. "Why me?"

Charlotte took a deep breath, a beat or two of silence hanging between us. I felt like I lived and died in those seconds. A familiar fight-or-flight instinct kicked up inside me. Like I could sense an electrical storm coming, the hairs on the back of my neck standing up. The next thing she said changed my life forever. "You have a daughter, Gabe. She's not quite six months old, and her name is Savannah."

"What?" I said, for lack of anything better. Then, "Oh, fuck."

Way to be eloquent, dude.

"Look, I'm sorry to drop it on you like this," she said, though I was only half listening at that point, still reeling from the shrapnel of what she'd just told me. "And technically there's a chance the baby isn't yours. I mean, Alexis wasn't sure who the father was when she arrived here in Harpers Ferry, but..." She hesitated. "Well, she's got your ears, Gabe. I'd recognize them anywhere."

Shit.

Self-conscious now, I ran my hand over the top of one. They *were* noticeable. I'd always known that. And they had this weird little fold thing at the top. All the Kelleys had them. Mom and Dad used to say they were a marker, the sign of a true Kelley. If the baby had them, then…

My heart dropped as I tried to take everything in. Okay. Maybe this was that kind of phone call after all.

Although not the way I'd imagined.

"I even pulled out our old high school yearbooks one time," Charlotte said. "To show Alexis and to double-check myself, and yep. They're the same." She sighed. In the background, I could hear what sounded like sirens. "Anyway, Alexis told me she'd come to Harpers Ferry because she was on the run. She said an abusive ex-boyfriend with major jealousy issues had put her in the hospital earlier in her pregnancy, and she refused to take any more chances with her baby's life. And now she's dead."

Her voice did catch on a sob then, and my heart twisted. It was too much to take in all at once.

"Seems like too much of a coincidence to me," she said, after a moment to collect herself.

"I don't believe in coincidences."

Just then the train pulled into the station with another loud blare of the horn and the high-pitched screeching of brakes. I felt overwhelmed, like the earth was rocking beneath my feet, but one thing was certain. I was getting on that last train to Harpers Ferry.

TWO

I 'd pushed memories of this place from my mind for years, but as the Uber traveled through my hometown, they came flooding back. It was small, only about three hundred residents, which meant everyone knew everyone else's business. Both a blessing and a curse.

We headed down the wide main street, lined on both sides by stone buildings and storefronts. The old hardware store was still there, as was the diner. I remembered they had really good pancakes and hash browns. Some new places too. A coffee shop. A sporting goods store that seemed to cater to the tourists who stopped here on their way to climb or hike. Beyond town was lots of scenic area to bike or hike or fish or simply get lost in nature. In fact, the whole area was basically national parks.

The red brick exterior of Rhodes Tavern, where I was meeting Charlotte, matched the town's historic feel, but it looked different than I remembered from high school. It had been renovated, and around the side I could see what looked like a large patio. Getting approval for any changes to the old buildings around here practically took an act of

Congress, so whoever owned this place obviously knew what they were doing.

I went inside and walked up to the bar. "I'm here to see Charlotte Rhodes, please."

"Sure," the guy said. "Just a minute. I'll let her know you're here. Can I get you a drink first?"

"No, thanks."

I propped myself on a stool and dropped my duffel bag at my feet, still trying to process what Charlotte had told me on the phone. The air smelled of alcohol and fried food. My stomach rumbled. I hadn't eaten since lunch, but that could wait until after we figured out what the hell was going on.

"She's right over there," the bartender said as he returned.

I looked to where he was pointing at the back of the bar, and there stood Charlotte halfway down a hallway, looking pretty much the same as I remembered. Well, except for the baby carrier over her arm. Same long, sandy brown hair. Same hazel-green eyes. Same tall, lithe, graceful build.

Fuck.

Reality slapped me upside the head. This was real. This was happening. That could very well be my kid. Pulse racing like a thoroughbred, I slid off my stool and wove through the crowded bar toward Charlotte, my gaze flicking between her and the baby carrier. I couldn't see the kid yet, but I realized I'd made a mistake about Charlotte. She wasn't the same as I remembered. Back in high school, she'd been cute. Now she was a total knockout.

"Gabe?" The way her eyes widened slightly as she looked me over told me she must've been surprised at how I'd turned out too. My gaze flicked down to the beauty mark near the corner of her mouth, then up to the tiny diamond twinkling from her pierced nose. I found both of those things way hotter than I should have.

A bit flustered, I nodded and took a step forward, only to stop again at the sound of an infant gurgling. The world narrowed to just that hallway, just that moment.

The baby's face was still hidden by the carrier and the blankets. Part of me didn't want to see her. But then a tiny, pink-sock-covered foot kicked in the air and something inside me melted.

Oh God.

Charlotte gave me a shaky smile, and I realized I was staring, but I couldn't help it. There was too much to process. She could very well be holding my *child*. Out of nowhere she burst into tears, and I snapped back into the present, ready to work.

I took a deep breath. This was a crisis. An emergency. I was trained to deal with these. I could do this. I walked over and put my arm around her shoulders. "Is there somewhere quiet we can talk?" I asked.

She nodded and led me back down the hall to her office, leaning against me for support. It put me closer to the baby and to her and allowed me to finally get a glimpse inside the carrier. To say I was enchanted at first sight is cliché, but damn. I was. Little Savannah was the spitting image of me. And yep. Charlotte was right. She had the Kelley ears too.

My heart stuttered, pinching hard. I remembered how my dad, who we'd inherited those ears from, always used to try to hide his under hats. Remembered the first time I'd seen my younger brother, Isaac, after they brought him home from the hospital, and running my finger over the top of his ear. Same as mine. A mark of true brothers.

A mark of *family*.

God, I missed them so much.

Stuffing all those emotions down deep, I got on with it. I managed to get Charlotte into her office and settled at a small table there with the baby before closing the door and taking a seat across from her.

"I'm sorry for falling apart on you like that," she said, sniffling into a tissue from a box she pulled out of her desk drawer. "It's been a hell of a night."

"I understand." In situations like this, I found letting the other person talk, in their own time, was best, so I waited.

Finally, after blowing her nose and sipping from a bottle of water, Charlotte gave me a rundown of what had happened earlier. "After I tried to get ahold of Alexis for hours, I finally went and picked Savannah up at the sitter's myself. When I took her home, I found the cops swarming the place and..." She swallowed hard and looked away, pulling another tissue from the box before continuing. "The police said they think she was a victim of a break-in gone wrong, but that doesn't sit right with me. Not after some of the stuff she told me."

I started to ask what that stuff was, but the baby started fussing.

Charlotte reached over to shush her, soft and sad. "She's going to miss her mama. Aren't you, baby girl?" She straightened and met my gaze. "They put Savannah in my care for the time being. I was Alexis's birthing partner, and I'm Savannah's godmother." She cleared her throat. "I'm also a registered foster mother. Alexis encouraged me to do it." She threw her hands up, one still clutching her tissue. "God, it's like she'd been setting all this up since she arrived or something. Like she knew this was going to happen."

Her pretty face dissolved into tears again, and I stared at the floor until she collected herself, not wanting to embarrass her. Then the baby wailed, and Charlotte focused on rocking Savannah in her carrier, easing the awkwardness between us at last.

"I need to get her home soon," she said, not looking at me. "So I can feed her. But first, she needs to be changed."

"Right." That was my cue to leave. "I should go too. I need to find a hotel room." I pushed to my feet and picked up my duffel bag, slinging it over my shoulder and giving a self-conscious laugh. "To tell you the truth, I wasn't even sure I was going to get on the train and come back here, before you called."

"Really?" She looked up at me, her hazel eyes bright in the dim room.

"Yeah." We looked at each other for a second, and something passed between us before I turned away. "Anyway, I'll call around for a reservation. We can hash the rest of this out in the morning."

My hand was on the door handle when she said from behind me, "Don't be silly. You can stay at my place tonight. I've got plenty of room, and that way you can spend some time with Savannah too."

I turned, opening my mouth to decline, but noticed that she was hugging herself tightly and still seemed to be trembling. Then I thought about what it must've been like for her to discover her friend had been killed.

As if confirming my thoughts, she said, "I'd feel better having someone there, just in case."

That did it. She'd uncovered my kryptonite, hinting that she felt like she needed protection. Staying in a virtual stranger's house wasn't my usual MO, but we had known each other as kids, so it wasn't totally random. And it would be nice to have more time to get to know my daughter.

"Okay, then," I agreed. "I'll stay with you. Just for tonight."

"Good." Charlotte smiled, and I felt like I'd done my job. I swallowed hard. "Let me get the baby ready, and we can go."

THREE

Poor Savannah was screaming by the time we pulled into my driveway. I'd been chattering on for what felt like forever, trying to fill the conversational void between me and Gabe as we drove toward my house, but now the baby took precedence.

"Is she hurt?" he asked, looking back over his shoulder at Savannah, his expression a mix of worry and wariness. "She's screaming like she's hurt."

"She's fine. It's late, and she's hungry and exhausted, that's all," I assured him. I cut the engine, then got out and opened the back driver's side door to get Savannah's car seat. "If you could grab the diaper bag and carry it inside for me, that would be great."

"Sure thing," he said, gathering his duffel bag and her diaper bag. I handed him the keys, too, since my hands were full with Savannah's carrier. Gabe let us into the house, and I switched on the lights, glad that I'd managed to pick up a little this morning before work, so the place was less messy than usual.

"Make yourself comfortable," I said, walking toward the makeshift nursery I'd set up in a corner of my bedroom, down the hall. I was glad for the baby care to keep my mind off everything else for a few minutes. "Let me get her into a fresh onesie, and then we can talk." As I went, I flipped on lights in all the rooms, feeling better when the shadows were gone. I knew it was silly, but after what happened to Alexis…

I shuddered. In my room, I lifted Savannah out of her carrier and held her in front of me. She gave me one of her adorable, wobbly baby smiles, and a tsunami of emotion washed over me again. Holding Savannah close, I walked the perimeter of the room, murmuring to her and telling her it would be okay—as much for myself as for her. "We're going to be fine. Yes, we are."

Now, if only I could make myself believe it, we'd be all set.

I'd never lost anyone like this before. So sudden. So wrong. I wasn't sure what I was supposed to do. Then a hint of a dirty diaper made that decision for me.

It was good. Routine. Stopped me from thinking so much. I quickly got Savannah cleaned and changed, then dressed in a fresh onesie for bed. Now, time for a bottle.

I turned to head back out to the kitchen, only to freeze.

Gabe stood in the doorway, his gaze fixed on Savannah. How could such a tall, muscular guy look absolutely terrified of a tiny baby?

"I need to feed her," I said softly. "Want to help me give her a bottle?"

"Uh." He scrubbed a hand over the top of his short, dark hair, then ducked his head. Everything about the man seemed spring-loaded and made of muscle, but the move was a tell, a hint that maybe, beneath the tough-guy facade, Gabe wasn't quite the powerhouse he seemed to be.

Right now he had a lost-puppy look about him, and I'd always been a sucker for that, so I gestured for him to follow me. We went back to the kitchen, and I pulled the can of formula and an empty bottle from the diaper bag. I would've handed him the baby to hold while I mixed it up, but I was afraid he'd pass out cold on me, and there was no way I could move him myself.

He towered over me, and it wasn't like I was petite. The way that drab green T-shirt clung to his cut torso in all the right places was probably illegal in several states. Not overly sculpted, like a gym rat, but honest muscle, honed by hard work.

Oh God. Stop looking. Stop looking.

I focused instead on mixing up the formula, then heating it in the microwave.

"Your place is nice," he said, for lack of anything better, I suppose.

"Thanks." It wasn't that nice. I'd bought it cheap and fixed it up when I could. It was better than when I'd bought it—the kitchen had been redone, and the hardwood floors gleamed—but most importantly, it was mine. The microwave beeped, and I pulled out the bottle, testing a drop on my wrist before turning back to Gabe. Savannah squirmed in my arms, already reaching for the bottle. She was probably starving, poor thing. Between the police station and the bar, it was way past her usual feeding time.

Gabe was still looking at us like we were from another planet, curious and cautious, but enough was enough. If he was going to be Savannah's dad, he needed to get used to her.

I hiked my chin toward a stool at the granite-topped breakfast bar. "Take a seat, and I'll hand her to you."

"Oh, uh…" For a second, I thought he might bolt, but then he gave a curt nod and took a seat like I'd given him an order. Good man. I walked over and stood in front of him, setting the bottle on the bar.

"Okay. Have you held a baby before?"

"Yeah. But it's been a while."

"Okay. Well, pretend she's a football, then," I said, falling back on my foster mother training. "You want to cradle her body with your arm, supporting her neck and back. And you'll want to keep her tilted while she eats. Otherwise it could all come back up, and nobody wants that. Trust me."

Gabe gave a nervous chuckle, his eyes locked on Savannah. "Got it. I'm ready."

"Good." I waited until he'd moved his arms into position, then slowly transferred the baby to him. The look on Gabe's face, the way it shifted from fear to fascination to wonder, nearly made me cry all over again, but in a good way this time. I stepped back and smiled. "Say hi to your baby daughter."

I couldn't stop staring at her. This tiny human. I'd made this. Maybe. There was still a slight possibility that she wasn't my daughter, but… I looked at those ears again.

Nope. No way. Those were Kelley ears, and she was definitely mine.

Charlotte walked out into the living room and grabbed a throw pillow from the sofa, then returned to shove it under my arm for support. That helped. More comfortable. Not that Savannah weighed a lot. She felt like nothing in my arms. Nothing and everything, all at the same time.

A knot of panic clogged my throat again.

Oh God. The baby's survival depended on me right now. In my mind, Savannah suddenly went from being a baby to being a live grenade— just as delicate and prone to explode at my slightest mistake. The bottle popped out of her tiny pink mouth, and her bottom lip quivered in the saddest pout I'd ever seen. A total punch to the heart.

"Put the bottle back to her lips," Charlotte said. I did, and the pout disappeared beneath a barrage of noisy sucking. It was so cute, I couldn't help but laugh.

"She's a good eater," I said.

"Yep. She is," Charlotte agreed. "Her favorite is pancakes in the morning." At my confused look—as far as I could see, there weren't any teeth in that tiny mouth yet—Charlotte chuckled. "The frozen kind. Alexis used to buy the small ones at the grocery store, then tear them up into teeny pieces for her. They're soft, so she doesn't choke on them, and the coldness soothes her gums when they're sore from teething."

Ah. Right. That answered the teeth question. I nodded and looked back down at Savannah. "I'd like to see her eat them sometime."

"Well, you should—" Charlotte started, only to stop when Savannah swallowed an air bubble and started to choke. We both moved at the same time, me more on instinct than anything, since I had little to no experience with babies. The last time I'd held one this long had been when Isaac was born. My stomach dropped, and I put Savannah over my shoulder, patting her tiny back to ease her coughing. Finally it stopped, and I looked up at Charlotte, who was watching us closely.

"You're a natural," she said.

I wasn't. Proved by the fact that, the minute I tried to lower the baby back down to feed her again, I was all thumbs. It was typical of me.

Great in a crisis, not always so great at everyday life situations. Logistically, my problem was figuring out how to get Savannah from my shoulder to the crook of my elbow without dropping her. Then there was the fact that I'd set the bottle down and it had rolled out of reach. Shit. To top things off, the baby was pouting again, which quickly escalated to a full-blown, ear-splitting wail.

Fuck. I'd been doing this dad stuff for less than an hour, and already I was failing.

"Here," Charlotte said, swooping in to my rescue. She reached over and adjusted Savannah in my arms, then handed me the bottle. "You're doing great."

It didn't feel that way. I sighed. "Do you want to take her?"

"I think you should keep going. I'll do the burping afterward."

Bottle done, Charlotte was as good as her word and took Savannah away from me. I sat in the chair, watching her walk the baby around the perimeter of the kitchen and living room, cooing to her and getting her settled to sleep.

"Small steps," I said, feeling useless as I watched a pro at work. Like I knew what the hell I was talking about. But still, she was my kid, and my instincts hadn't led me wrong so far. Or, at least, it felt like she was my kid. I wanted proof, tangible proof, even if there was a connection there regardless. "I wonder how long DNA test results take," I said, thinking out loud.

My original plan had been to come home, visit the cemetery, put flowers on my family's graves and make my peace with it, then return to my SEAL team. I'd taken a week of leave. But now things had changed. First thing I'd need to do was move back my return date. It shouldn't be a problem. I had plenty of time to take, since I never went on leave. No need, with nothing to come back to. A day here and there, sure, to blow off steam, but nothing longer. Not in ten years. But now…

Charlotte gave me a look from across the room—not angry, exactly, but definitely upset.

Shit. Had I said some of that out loud too? Apparently.

Well, there was nothing I could do about it. I had to make plans. I couldn't just go AWOL.

FOUR

"Come on, sleepy girl," I said, carrying Savannah down the hall to my bedroom. "Let's get you into bed." I lowered her into the pack and play I used for a crib whenever she and Alexis came over, then straightened, arranging the blanket over her so she wouldn't get cold.

God. The thought of poor Alexis made my chest clench with grief. I looked up at the ceiling and whispered, "I'll take care of her, I promise. Whatever it takes, I'll do it."

Then I gazed back down at the baby, already sleeping soundly. She looked so peaceful and adorable it made my heart ache. I blinked hard, getting myself together. I wouldn't fall apart. I *couldn't*. Savannah needed me, and there was too much to do.

I needed to get the baby more clothes. And supplies. And toys. I should write this down so I didn't forget, my brain already filled with things I needed to do for the tavern. At least the baby had a safe place to sleep and me to take care of her. Hopefully, that would be enough until we got the rest figured out.

I headed back to the living room for paper and a pen and found Gabe at the kitchen table, still sitting exactly where I'd left him earlier, looking about as shellshocked as I felt. Poor guy. He'd had his entire world rocked in the span of about three hours. Taking pity on him, I wandered over and opened the fridge. "Are you hungry? Want something to drink?"

It took him a moment to respond. "I have some questions."

"Okay." I took a seat across from him and picked up my phone. "Let me order us a pizza first, since I haven't eaten all day."

Usually, I just popped a frozen one in the oven, but since Gabe was here, I figured I'd splurge on delivery. When I put the phone down, I clasped my hands atop the table, feeling out of sorts. Not defensive, exactly, but... wary. Yep. Wary was a good word for it. I hadn't seen this guy since high school, and I didn't like the way he made me feel... *studied*. Like he was sizing me up, even though I was the one who'd been here all along. "Okay. You've got thirty minutes. Ask away."

"When did Alexis come here?" He shifted in the chair to face me, tiny lines of tension near the corners of his mouth. Strangely enough, it only made him hotter. Not that I was looking, because I wasn't. Nope. "I met her last June in DC when I was on leave, but she told me she was from Pennsylvania, not West Virginia."

Right. *Focus, Charlotte. Focus.*

I coughed, then nodded. "Alexis came into Rhodes Tavern ten months ago, already four months pregnant, looking for a job. We became friends." I twitched slightly from the sudden stab of grief in my chest at the reminder that she was gone. "Best friends. Like sisters, really. We told each other everything. She didn't seem to have anyone else. One night, Alexis told me about her ex-boyfriend who beat her up and put her in the hospital, threatened her, stalked her." Describing it now made what happened to her seem even more inevitable. "Then, another time, she told me about this sweet Navy SEAL she'd met one night after she and her ex had broken up. She said she hoped you were Savannah's father."

Gabe shook his head, then raked a hand through his hair, like he was still having a hard time wrapping his head around it all. I couldn't say I blamed him. I was a mess at the moment too. "I don't know about the sweet part," he said. "But I remember that night. We had a great, uh, connection." He blushed. "The next morning, her phone kept blowing up with calls and texts from her ex, and I got out of there. Didn't want all that drama on leave, you know?" His expression clouded over with regret. "Jesus. Why the hell did I walk away?"

"Hey, you didn't know." Without thinking, I reached across the table to take his hand. He looked so distraught that it was easy to sympathize with the guy. My fingertips tingled from the heat of his skin, but I didn't move away. "It wasn't your fault."

"No," he said, staring down at the table. "But I feel like I could've done *something*. And then maybe things would be different?"

Our eyes locked, but I shook my head. I couldn't let him take the blame.

"Stop. Don't beat yourself up." I sat back, letting him go and crossing my arms, more in self-defense than anything else. Touching him had been a mistake, since now I seemed to be even more aware of him. I needed to forget this ridiculous zing through my bloodstream. It was distracting, and we had serious things to discuss.

We sat for a moment in silence, time stretching as we took in everything that had happened and everything that was left unanswered. I picked at the edge of the wooden table, frowning. "The police let me into Alexis's house earlier, to grab some extra diapers and stuff for Savannah for the next few days. It was a mess. But considering it was supposed to be a robbery, I thought it was weird that whoever it was —the person who killed her—didn't take her laptop. It was new and expensive and sitting right there on the coffee table." I squeezed my eyes shut, remembering that awful scene. "What was even weirder, though, was that right beside the computer were a bunch of smashed picture frames, mainly with pictures of Alexis and Savannah in them. Seemed pretty random for a thief with no connection to the victim, right?"

I paused a moment before putting words to my darkest fear about all this, the one that had haunted me since I'd pulled up at the crime scene. I whispered it, low and rough from lack of oxygen, because suddenly it was hard to breathe. "What if her ex found her?"

Gabe studied me, then reached over and took my hand, his fingers strong and warm around mine. "Hey, it's going to be okay."

The way he said it almost made me believe him.

"I'm going to talk to my CO and see if I can extend my leave," he continued. "We'll get this all figured out, I promise."

After dinner, Charlotte got me set up in the guest bedroom down the hall from hers. At first I thought it was silly that she locked her bedroom door behind her, since just about anyone could kick the damned thing in and be done with it, but I understood her need to feel secure. Then I took another look at the door to my own room and realized how solidly the house was built. None of those flimsy locks you can twist open with a table knife. That was good, though I could protect her and the baby better than any lock.

I spent more time than necessary unpacking, because the routine of it calmed me and helped me think through things. Besides, I liked to stay organized. They'd trained us that way in boot camp, and I'd gotten used to it. Order made sense to me. Once I got my stuff put away, I pulled out my phone and called my CO. It was way early where the guys were right now, but given the situation, he'd understand.

"Smith here," my CO answered after two rings. He sounded groggy.

"Hey, sir. It's Gabe. I'm sorry to bother you so early in the morning, but I've got a situation here." I filled him in on everything I knew, then said, "I can't leave them like this, sir."

"No. I get that," Smith said. "Stay there and do what you need to do, Kelley. Help them if you can. But keep me posted. And if you need us for anything, call. I'll put in a request to extend your leave."

"Thanks, sir," I said, relieved, and started to end the call.

"What are your plans for your little girl?" he asked, getting to the heart of the matter before I could hang up.

"Uh…" I wasn't sure what to say. Hadn't really gotten that far yet. "I'm not sure, sir."

I knew deployments couldn't accommodate babies, but if I got stationed on a base, maybe I could have a kid with me. The last thing I wanted to do was become part of Savannah's life, only to walk away again. It wouldn't be fair to her. But I also didn't want to leave until things were settled here, which could take days or weeks. It was all still up in the air.

God, this was awful. I sank down on the edge of the bed, the past crowding in on my present. Being back here, holding the baby, brought back all my memories of Mom and Dad. Of Isaac. I didn't want to deal with any of that right now, those dark feelings sucking me down into a black hole of grief and despair, the wound in my heart never quite healing. But I couldn't ignore it either. Not anymore.

29

"I do think it's good that I came home to Harpers Ferry," I said eventually. "For a lot of reasons. I've got unfinished business here I need to put to rest."

"Well, like I said, we'll be here for you if you need us once you figure it out, Kelley," Smith said. "Keep us in the loop."

The call ended then, and I changed, then shut off the lights and flopped back onto the bed, staring up at the ceiling. But the mattress was too soft. It almost made me laugh, the idea that comfort didn't work for me.

Yet another part of my life that wouldn't make sense to anyone else. I was used to sleeping on the ground or stealing a few minutes of shut-eye in transit, so I ended up pulling a blanket and pillow off the bed and stretching out on the floor.

I closed my eyes and tried to force the tension from my shoulders. I felt like I hadn't rested in days, yet when my thoughts drifted to the sweet baby just down the hall from me, I knew sleep wouldn't come for a long time.

FIVE

I tiptoed down the hall, hoping I wouldn't wake either of my houseguests. I needed some quiet time alone to work through the chaos that had been thrown in my lap the day before. My heart pinched at the reason for it. *Alexis.*

I was going to make everything right. For her, and for her beautiful daughter.

Gabe's door was cracked open, and I couldn't stop myself from peeking in. Based on the snoring, it was clear that he'd needed a good night's sleep. My eyes fell on the unmade bed—which was empty. I pushed the door farther open and stepped inside to try to figure out what was going on. I was greeted by the sight of Gabe asleep on his side on the floor, the blanket half off his body. How was it possible that he actually looked *comfortable* on the hard wood?

His face was smashed into the pillow, and his forehead was furrowed, like he was at work even in his dreams. For a second I imagined slipping closer to him to pull the blanket up over his shoulder and whisper that everything was going to be okay.

Not that I could promise any such thing. Hell, nothing made sense to me at the moment. Not the child sleeping a few feet away or the handsome mountain snoring on the ground.

As I stood there, Gabe's eyes snapped open abruptly, like he'd felt the weight of my gaze.

"Oh!" I managed, backing toward the door. "I, uh, the *bed*. I didn't know where you, uh, so I came in and, um…"

Gabe's sleepy face transformed with a smile as I stuttered.

"I'm sorry!"

I turned and jogged down the hall, feeling my cheeks burning.

In the kitchen, I made breakfast to distract myself. I brewed coffee, fried eggs, and buttered toast, praying that by the time Gabe appeared, I wouldn't feel like such an ass. But no such luck.

"Hey," he said, walking into the kitchen, looking casually gorgeous in a black T-shirt and faded jeans with his feet bare and hair damp from his shower. "Uh, about the bedroom. I'm sorry if I scared you or whatever." He did the hair-raking thing again, which I found adorable… and irritating because it was adorable. "I have trouble sleeping on a soft bed. I'm not used to it anymore. When I'm on missions we usually sleep on a cot or the ground, so…"

Well, that made sense, then. And now I felt sorry for him on top of everything else. Imagining him sleeping on the cold, hard ground with the bugs and the critters and… ugh. I grabbed some plates from the cupboard and began serving up the food. I started asking questions, afraid if I didn't we'd lapse into awkward silence. "What about when you come home on leave?"

"Thank you for this," he said, taking the full plates and setting them on the table. "I don't come home often, to be honest. Since I don't really have a home to come to anymore. I mainly stay in hotels when I do, and, yeah, sometimes I end up on the floor. I've got some friends in DC I sometimes crash with, and they're used to my quirks."

I handed him a mug and pointed to the coffee maker. "Grab some, and let's eat before Savannah wakes up. She'll sleep off her four a.m. bottle any time now. She's nothing if not a good little eater."

"Takes after her daddy then," he said, chuckling. He fixed his coffee, then took a seat across from me at the table to eat. He was right: Savannah did take after him, appetite-wise. He managed to down pretty much all the food I'd made, with the exception of what I had on my plate. I wasn't sure exactly where he put it, since there didn't appear to be any spare fat on him. I concentrated on my food, and we made small talk as he checked his phone. For a little while, everything felt... normal.

My phone rang as Gabe got up to clear the table. I stared down at the number for the social worker handling Savannah's case on my caller ID, and my heart raced. "Hello?"

"Ms. Rhodes," the social worker said. "This is Mrs. Thompson, from the Bureau for Children and Families. I'm calling to let you know that a new petition for custody has been made in the Savannah Barnes case, on the grounds that he's her biological father. It's by a man named Elijah Harris. Do you know him?"

My fingers went numb, and I nearly dropped my phone. I sank down on the living room couch, light-headed.

"Uh, yes. I know him," I managed to say. "I mean, I know of him. Alexis talked about him."

The social worker then rattled on about what would happen now that there'd been a paternity claim made, but I only half listened, my thoughts snarled into a knot. Finally, she said goodbye, and I ended the call with shaking fingers. Jesus. Alexis's ex had filed a custody claim for Savannah. But why? He'd have to show reasonable

33

evidence that he was connected to Alexis and could have fathered her baby, and Alexis had told me that she knew in her heart that Gabe was the father, so…

Oh God.

"Hey, where do you—" Gabe asked, walking up beside me. My inner turmoil must've shown on my face, because next thing I knew, he'd crouched down and covered my shaking, icy hands with his warm, steady ones. "What's wrong?"

I swallowed hard, my mouth and throat so dry I could hardly spit out the words. But he needed to know. "It's Alexis's ex," I croaked out. "He's coming for Savannah. The social worker said he petitioned the court for custody."

Gabe went silent, his expression hardening until he growled, feral and possessive. Under different circumstances, I would've found it hot. I liked guys who were a bit alpha. Right then, though, I was just thankful for the support. "I won't let him touch a hair on Savannah's head," he said. "I swear. We'll sort this out."

A few hours later, after we'd gotten the baby up and fed and bathed, we loaded Savannah into the car and took off for the Jefferson County Courthouse. I did my best to act normal, but inside I was scared to death. There was no way I was letting Alexis's ex take custody of her child. I blinked at the road as I drove, my eyes stinging.

No. We wouldn't let that happen. That was why we were going to the courthouse: so Gabe could put in his own petition for custody. He could prove once and for all that Savannah was his, and no one could ever take her away again. Especially not someone who was capable of… well, I wasn't ready to go there yet.

Gabe sat in the passenger seat, a muscle ticking near his tense jaw. He couldn't seem to sit still, fiddling with the radio, then the window, then his phone. I knew the feeling. I wanted to ask him more about his family, since he never really talked about them, but I didn't feel comfortable enough to do that yet. It had to be hard for him, I supposed, not having anyone else in the world. My mom and I didn't always get along well, but I knew she was there for me all the same.

My thoughts went back to high school, when Gabe had been Mr. Popular. Quarterback, swim team captain, dating a cheerleader. We hadn't really hung out in the same circles, but I still felt like I knew him, in a way. Then the accident had happened, and it was like he'd changed into a different person overnight. Became more serious and withdrawn. Of course, losing his family and his home would do that.

I remembered being in a math class with him, and where he'd always been the first to answer questions—because he was smart, too—but after the accident he never raised his hand anymore. Just sat there, frowning down at his desk, probably dreaming of the day he could get the hell out of Harpers Ferry and away from all the pain the place held for him now. Apparently I'd been right, since he'd gone away a few days after graduation and never returned. Until now.

"Hey," I said, turning down the radio he'd cranked up seconds earlier. "It's going to be all right. Isn't that what you told me?"

He shrugged, staring out the window beside him, muttering, "Dammit, I should've come here yesterday and started the process."

I shook my head and sighed. "The offices were closed long before you even got to town. Besides, I don't think it would've mattered, Gabe. The court doesn't care who got there first. That's not how it works. And I doubt it would've stopped Alexis's ex from filing. The social worker assured me that she wouldn't remove Savannah from my care until the DNA tests came back, anyway."

There was no way in hell I was letting that abusive asshole take Savannah from me. None.

Fear burned inside me like acid. I couldn't even imagine a scenario where Gabe wasn't the baby's father, because that would be… wrong.

I mean, there was no proof her ex had been involved in Alexis's death. But even if he hadn't killed her and it was some random act of violence, he'd frightened and harassed her, and that was unacceptable. I refused to turn over sweet Savannah to him without a fight.

I must've sped up as my anger built, because next thing I knew, Gabe was leaning over to peer at the speedometer.

"Uh, you might want to slow down there," he said, giving me some side-eye. "It won't help anyone if we're arrested for reckless driving and endangering a minor. We've got time."

Do we? I wanted to yell but didn't. He was right. I looked in the rearview mirror at Savannah sleeping peacefully in her car seat and knew I'd do anything for her. Anything.

A short time later, we pulled into the courthouse parking lot and I cut the engine. Gabe and I gave each other nods that seemed to say we were ready to head into battle together. I wasn't the sort of teammate he was used to, but I'd show him I could hold my own. When it came to the baby, I was ready to go full mama bear.

Gabe went over to speak with the clerk, and I stood next to him, cradling Savannah in my arms. The woman's eyes jumped from him to me, then to the baby. I wondered what she thought about us. Did she know the details of the case, or did she think we were involved in some daytime television paternity scandal?

Savannah looked like the man I knew was her father, but could the clerk tell that I was nothing more than a glorified babysitter? I shook my head. No. I was Savannah's *godmother*. I mattered.

The baby sighed and rested her head on my shoulder as if she'd heard my thoughts. I kissed her soft hair, and Gabe glanced at me, his eyes gentle.

The clerk looked everything over and stamped a few forms before handing them to Gabe.

"You'll need to submit to a DNA test, and it will take a few weeks to get the results," the clerk said, her expression pinched. "I hope you'll react better to that news than the last man who was here. Our lab is backed up at the moment, and there's nothing we can do about it, I'm afraid."

Gabe's hands tightened on the documents at the mention of Elijah. I jumped in. "As long as Savannah won't be removed from my care until the results are back, I'm fine with it." I looked at Gabe, and he nodded. "I mean, *we're* fine with it."

The clerk assured me everything would remain the same, so we gathered our things to head out.

We walked down the hallway in silence, and when we stepped outside, I felt like I could breathe again.

SIX

I didn't end up getting my blood drawn until three days later.

By the time we left the courthouse, Savannah was getting fussy, ready for her feeding, so we headed back to Charlotte's place. Then the lab was closed for the weekend, and I had to watch the baby while Charlotte worked at the tavern, so yeah. Monday it was.

Now, as I drove by myself through the Appalachian Mountains back toward Charles Town, I was struck again by how pretty it was here. Especially this time of year, when the leaves were starting to turn. The fall colors reminded me how much I appreciated the change of seasons. No matter how far work took me from my home, this place would aways be in my blood.

The lab was in a brick building a few streets down from the courthouse, and I parallel parked at the curb before going inside. There was a sterile waiting room that smelled faintly of antiseptic and bleach. It reminded me of a military clinic. Going overseas, it seemed like I was constantly getting a shot for something or other. I was more than used to medical waiting rooms.

After I checked in with the receptionist, I took a seat and scrolled through my phone. Nothing worked to quiet the noise in my head. What I was about to do could change the course of my life.

I felt eyes on me and looked up to see a gray-haired woman staring at me. It took me a second to process why.

"Gabe? Is that you?"

I jumped out of my chair, feeling my face go hot. "Yes, ma'am, it's me. Been a long time."

Too long.

Mrs. Kepner took me in and kept me in school after my family died so I could finish my senior year, a neighbor who went far out of her way to help me. She'd been one of my champions back then, but I hadn't seen or spoken to her since I left for the Navy.

"Don't you 'ma'am' me! Get over here." She smiled warmly as she took me into an embrace.

She felt thinner than I remembered, and smaller. She let me go, then looked me over. "You look great, Gabe," she said, smiling. "I always wondered how you made out after you left Harpers Ferry."

I felt guilty for not keeping in touch with her after all she'd done for me, but when I'd left this place behind, I'd left for good. Or so I thought. Now, I realized I'd done so at the expense of all the people who'd helped me through the darkest period of my life. Heat prickled my cheeks as I apologized. "I'm sorry, Mrs. Kepner. Things were rough back then, and I was young and stupid and—"

"Sweetheart, stop," she said, holding up a hand. "I understand."

"Well, thank you for everything you did for me." I wasn't sure I'd ever said those words to her before, but I wanted her to know now. "I wouldn't be here now if it wasn't for you."

Mrs. Kepner patted my cheek. "You're very welcome, Gabe. And you could write to me once in a while, you know. My address hasn't changed."

"Okay," I said, still blushing. "I promise I will."

"Mr. Kelley?" the receptionist called. "The lab tech is ready for you now."

"Guess that's me," I said, stating the obvious. "See you later."

"I hope I do," Mrs. Kepner said, holding my gaze.

The receptionist pointed me toward a door on the right, and I went through into a small white room with a chair and a table covered in phlebotomy supplies—tubes, needles, rubber tourniquets, alcohol pads, cotton balls. The tech confirmed my name and Social Security number, then told me to have a seat.

"Good veins," she said, eyeing the twisty blue lines on the inside of my arm as she tied the rubber tourniquet around my bicep. "You look like you work out."

I grunted. I wasn't in the mood to get into my background.

She was good and got my sample on one stick with the needle. I was done in a snap.

"Thanks so much," I said, standing to pull my jacket back on. "When should the results be in?"

"Looks like they put a stat on these," the tech said, scanning her paperwork again. "But we're backed up, so I'd say two, maybe three weeks tops."

"Okay. Great. Thanks." I went back out into the waiting room, but it was empty now. I was hoping to see Mrs. Kepner, so I could thank her again, but she'd disappeared. I walked out into the sunny day, taking a deep breath of the fresh air, feeling somehow lighter than before as I headed back to Charlotte's place.

Maybe there was more to making peace with things here than simply visiting the cemetery.

"I'm on my way back now," Gabe said over the phone. "Want me to grab something for dinner?"

"No, don't bother, I can throw something together." There wasn't much in the fridge at present, since I hadn't made it to the grocery store yet this week. I wasn't used to feeding two adults, but I knew how to stretch a meal.

A loud knock sounded on the door. I wasn't expecting anybody. Frowning, I said, "Hey, someone's here. I need to go."

I heard him start to talk as I ended the call, and for a second I wished I hadn't hung up, so I wouldn't feel so alone when facing whoever was outside. To say I was nervous after what happened to Alexis would be putting it mildly. I hit pause on the microwave, where I was heating a bottle for Savannah, and walked over to the front door. Through the peephole, I spotted a state trooper on the porch and released my pent-up breath. Okay. So, not a stalker ex there to kill me and steal the baby.

Still, I left the chain on just to be safe as I opened the door. "Can I help you?"

"Yes, ma'am," the trooper said, tipping his hat to me. "My name's Elijah Harris, and I'd like to see my daughter."

I blinked at him a moment, taking that in as adrenaline flooded my system.

Shit. Shit, shit, shit.

It was the stalker ex. Dressed as a cop. Or maybe he really was a cop. I didn't know. Didn't care. All I knew was that I was there alone with Savannah, and this asshole would never get his hands on her. Never. My legs felt weak, and if I hadn't had the doorframe to help hold me up, I would've collapsed on the floor. Thank God I'd left the chain on. Thank. God.

"Uh, I'm sorry. That's not possible," I said, hoping my voice wasn't shaking as badly as my insides. "She's not here."

Please don't cry, baby. Please don't cry.

From what the social worker had told me, placements were not made public in cases like this, which meant he'd either been stalking me too or he'd used his law enforcement connections to get the information. Either way, it was illegal. And terrifying as fuck.

My chest constricted, and my stomach churned. I did my best to squash down the fear and put on a brave front, to stall him until— hopefully—Gabe got back. "How did you find me?"

He stepped closer, trying to intimidate me with his size and bulk. It worked. He was every bit as tall and broad as Gabe, with a bit more muscle packed on at the gym. Alexis had a type, that was for sure. He didn't answer my question, instead growling through the cracked door, "Go get my baby."

The thought of poor Savannah with this man gave me the courage I needed to hold my ground. "No. If the courts order me to turn the baby over to you, I will. Until then…" I wanted to say *fuck off* but bit my tongue. "Back off."

He exhaled slowly. "I'm trying to be nice here." His tone was sharp enough to cut steel. "You should keep that in mind."

My nails dug into the wood trim of the doorframe, and bile rose hot in my throat. But I couldn't back down. Wouldn't back down. For Savannah's sake. For Alexis. "I know who you are," I said, the words clawing out of me. "I know what you did."

Elijah's expression darkened, and he put his hand on the door as if he meant to push his way in. I braced my foot against the bottom of the wood, ready to go to battle for the little girl sleeping a few rooms away.

Just then, Gabe pulled into the driveway, and I wanted to cry with relief. Harris glared at the car and stepped back, now that he had an audience. His face changed, too, from angry and hateful to polite and stoic.

Asshole.

Gabe walked up to the porch, taking in the state trooper uniform and me cowering behind the still-chained door. "Hey, what's going on?"

"Nothing to worry about," Elijah said in a smooth voice, like he hadn't been threatening me seconds earlier. "We're through here. Have a good night, sir."

He brushed past Gabe and jogged down the stairs to the white SUV parked at the curb. Weird that he was in uniform but driving an unmarked car. I watched until he pulled away, unable to move, unable to breathe.

"What was that about?" Gabe asked, concern written all over his handsome face.

I slid the chain free, then hung heavily on the door as I opened it for him, still afraid my knees would give way.

"You need to tell me what's wrong," he said. He put his arm around my waist to help me over to the sofa. As soon as I was settled, he went back to lock the door before taking a seat beside me, taking my cold hands in his to warm them. "Who was that? Why was he here?"

"He's... he's Alexis's ex. His name is Elijah Harris."

"Shit, he's a *cop*?" Gabe shook his head. "That complicates things. Son of a bitch. I can't believe he had the balls to show up here."

"There's something not right about him, Gabe," I said, staring down at our entwined fingers, drawing strength from him. "It's like, when I looked into his eyes, they were dead."

He nodded and looked like he wanted to say more, but then Savannah wailed for her bottle and reality snapped back to normal. Thank heavens she'd managed to sleep through the confrontation.

"I have a bottle for her in the microwave," I said, not moving.

"I'll get it and feed her." Gabe stood. "You take a minute to catch your breath, and then I want you to tell me everything you can about that conversation. Every detail."

As he walked away down the hall, I went back to the door, double- and triple-checking to make sure it was secure.

SEVEN

Over the course of a few days, I managed to transition from a clumsy oaf who knew nothing about infants to a pretty competent baby whisperer. I could feed, change, and dress Savannah on my own, without any input from Charlotte.

Our arrangement was strange, sure, but we were making it work. I never imagined myself in this position, yet here I was with spit-up on the front of my shirt and a snuggly little one nestled on my shoulder. And I was comfortable with it. Hell, I was *good* at it.

Charlotte was rushing around, trying to finish getting dressed and eat breakfast at the same time, when her phone rang. I was sitting in the living room, doing my best not to eavesdrop, but it was kind of impossible in such a small area.

"Hey, Mom," she said, cradling the phone between her cheek and shoulder while she rummaged around in the fridge. "Now isn't really a great time. What? Oh."

I could tell from Charlotte's tone that whatever her mom had said wasn't good. I shifted on the sofa to look back over my shoulder into the kitchen. Charlotte was leaning her hips against the counter now and rubbing her temple while she frowned. Yep. Definitely not good.

Concerned, I stood and walked into the kitchen with Savannah and gave Charlotte an inquiring look, mouthing "What's wrong?"

She waved me off and turned to face the window over the sink. "Okay, well, it can't be helped. No, Mom. It's fine. I hope you feel better soon. I'll just need to rearrange some stuff on my schedule. Move that franchising meeting again and find someone to cover for me. It's fine. Seriously. You rest and take care of yourself. I'll call you later. Bye."

Once Charlotte ended the call, I asked, "What's going on? You've moved that meeting like twice already, right?"

Charlotte turned back to me, looking defeated. "Yeah, but Mom's got a cold and can't take Savannah today, so I don't really have a choice."

"I can take her," I offered.

"What?" Charlotte chuckled. "Uh, no. Thanks for the offer, but no."

"Why?" Now it was my turn to frown. "Look, I know it's hard to believe, and that I still sometimes act like I could break her if I hold her the wrong way, but I've learned a lot the past six days. I can handle it. You know it's true."

She blinked at me a moment, like she was considering it, then shook her head. "No. I can't ask you to do that. I'll get someone to cover my shifts today. One of my managers is usually willing to pick up some extra hours."

"What about the franchising meeting?"

Charlotte shrugged, reaching out to take Savannah's tiny hand. "I don't know. I wasn't really sure about that whole deal anyway. It's probably better if I put it off for now."

Yeah. I wasn't buying that. "Come on. Seriously. I can watch Savannah for a few hours. We'll be fine. Go do what you need to do." At Charlotte's incredulous look, I added, "We've come to an understanding, Savannah and me."

To prove my point, I waggled my brows at the kid, and she squealed, then reached for me, looking delighted. It was the most adorable thing I'd ever seen and made me feel all warm and fuzzy inside. Then I leaned in closer and tickled her cute little belly, and just like that, her happy squeal turned into a full-body laugh. Amazing. And damn if I wasn't proud as hell for having caused it. By the time I looked over at Charlotte again, she was smiling too.

After a deep breath, she said, "Fine. You can watch her. But you need to promise you'll call me if you need anything at all, okay?"

"Okay," I said, hiding my eye roll by kissing Savannah's soft cheek. "We got this, don't worry. Now finish getting dressed and get out of here. You'll be late."

I was feeling pretty good about everything as I gave Savannah a bottle, then changed her diaper before settling in to watch some morning TV while burping her. It couldn't be that hard, right? Feed her, change her, entertain her when needed, put her down for naps. Piece of cake. I'd faced down snipers and terrorists and dictators. I could handle one tiny baby girl.

Except it seemed like the minute Charlotte walked out the door, Savannah started getting fussy. And no matter what I did, she wouldn't stop whining and crying and generally being unhappy. Even my trademark eyebrow waggle and tickle didn't help. In fact, it felt like everything I tried only made it worse. I started to worry that maybe she was sick, but when I pressed my fingers to her forehead it felt fine. So what was the problem? And what the hell had I been thinking, telling Charlotte that I could handle everything? Maybe this hadn't been a good idea after all.

I stood and carried the baby around the house, rubbing her back. No. I wasn't a quitter, especially where my own child was concerned. We'd get through this. I just needed to figure it out. The moving seemed to help a little, as Savannah became distracted by the passing scenery. All right, then. If walking around the house was good, getting outside in the fresh air would be even better, right? So, a walk it was.

I remembered Charlotte mentioning something about Savannah liking to be in her stroller. That was good. I got us both ready to go, and we headed out of the house and into the sunshine. Savannah gave a happy squeal. Good. Good. Back on solid ground. Things were improving. My spirits lifted.

As I pushed the stroller down the block, I pointed stuff out to Savannah, talking to her like she understood every word I was saying. A short distance from the house was part of the Appalachian Trail that led down to the Shenandoah River. It was a beautiful day, sunny and warm for autumn, so we went for it.

The gurgle of water joined the chorus of songbirds in the air, and I inhaled deeply, catching the scent of leaves and moss and decaying wood. Sunlight, filtered through the leaves above, dappled the path. A memory flashed through my head: walking down here with my mom, when I was a kid. I'd forgotten this was her favorite walking path.

How the hell could I forget something like that? Man. My family had been gone ten years, and already the memories were slipping away from me. Stuff like the sound of my dad's voice, or my mom's laugh, or how my brother would always fold his candy wrappers into little squares before flicking them at me across the table.

God, I missed them all so much. I'd forgotten how much until I'd come back here.

I sighed and stared out at the river beyond the trail. It hurt, being back here, in a weird and wonderful way that threatened to pull me under as fast as any rip current in that rushing water before me. That's probably why I'd avoided coming home for so long.

Nothing to do about it now, though. I glanced down at the baby again.

At least Savannah seemed to love it all, quieting right down and staring up, wide-eyed, at everything from her stroller, occasionally gurgling at something or chewing on her fingers. Several people stopped to talk to her and smile at me. She was adorable, no doubt about it. I felt a swell of fatherly pride. It was hard to believe that less than a week ago I didn't even know she existed. Now, I couldn't imagine life without her.

We continued on down the trail, passing people and looking at the scenery. After about an hour or so, we stopped along the riverbank and I took a seat on an empty bench. I gazed down at Savannah, thinking about my mom and how much she would've loved her granddaughter. About how she would've brought her here for walks too. My chest squeezed with the sweetness and sorrow of it all.

Determined not to get caught up in that grief again, I stood and smiled down at the baby. "Come on, darlin'. Time to get you home for a nap, eh?"

My day at the bar passed in a blur, between getting things ready to open, then the busy lunch shift, and then the meeting with the franchisers. I kept checking my phone, thinking Gabe would call sooner or later with some issue with Savannah, but he never did. In fact, I was starting to worry about it, but then things got busy again and I never got around to checking on them.

He handled dangerous, top-secret missions. He could handle a baby.

Of course he could.

Couldn't he?

As I sat in the dreadfully boring franchise meeting, I couldn't help thinking about how things had changed over the past week. I'd loved Alexis. I missed her so much it felt like a part of my soul was gone. Having Gabe and Savannah around helped, though. I saw so much of Alexis in her daughter. Saw more and more of Gabe in there too. He was growing on me, I had to admit. Funny, smart, kind, considerate. Even if he was a complete non-option in the happily-ever-after department.

I snorted to myself and rubbed the bridge of my nose. God, the meeting must be melting my brain for me to even go there. I straightened in my seat and tried to pay attention to the presentation the men in suits sitting around me had put together. So far, from what I could tell, they wanted to take my gorgeous, historic pub and turn it into one of those "neighborhood"-type chain restaurants with a bunch of local crap on the walls and servers running around in striped shirts and suspenders, hawking food and drinks with names like Shenandoah Sliders or Mountaintop Mud Pie.

I knew I should at least listen to what they had to say. It made smart business sense. Franchising the pub could certainly make me more money. But I loved the place and hated the idea of it not being mine, so…

Rather than get more anxious about the presentation, I turned my attention to the rest of the bar. It was well past the lunch rush now, but even so, there were still tables filled and food cooking on the grill. The low hum of chatter droned over the country tune playing on the speaker system, and the aroma of seasoned French fries wafted toward me, making my mouth water. God, I loved this place.

The meeting finally wrapped up a bit after four, and I managed to shake hands and play nice without letting on how much they'd wasted my time. Once they were out the door, I checked in with my evening staff, then headed home to see how Gabe and Savannah had fared. Despite the franchise plans falling through, I was feeling pretty much at peace with everything... until I rounded the corner on my block and saw a cop car in my driveway.

Oh shit.

I hurried toward my house, my mind racing. Okay. It was only one squad car. That was good, right? If something horrific had happened, there'd be more. So many more. The night they'd found Alexis, it felt like there'd been hundreds of emergency vehicles filling up the street and the yard and...

Fear trickled down my neck like ice water. By the time I reached the house, I was all but running, out of breath and sweaty and shaking. I parked near the curb and got out, racing to the porch where Gabe stood talking to a uniformed officer. Savannah was in his arms, looking whole and unhurt, thank God.

The minute I stepped onto the porch, Gabe turned and handed the baby to me. Savannah gurgled and grinned, reaching up with her drool-covered hands to pat my cheeks like she could sense I needed reassurance. Through numb lips, I asked, "What's going on?"

Gabe took a deep breath. "We had a break-in. I took Savannah for a walk around the neighborhood this afternoon, and when we came back I found the house trashed."

My heart stopped and started again, tumbling over itself with adrenaline. How the hell could this happen?

Without waiting or asking the police officer for permission, I pushed past the men and walked into my living room. It looked like a bomb had gone off in there. Debris lay everywhere, the coffee table smashed in half. I peered into the kitchen and wished I hadn't. It was even worse in there.

Cabinet doors ripped off or hanging by a single hinge. Dishes shattered all over the floor. Drawers yanked out and tossed, their contents all over the countertops. Anger and the sense of being violated rolled through me in waves. What the actual fuck was happening here? I couldn't look at the rest of the house. Couldn't handle that. Not yet.

Savannah started fussing, picking up on my inner turmoil, and I stroked her back as I returned to the front porch, where Gabe and the officer waited. My face felt hot, and my mouth was dry. "How did this happen? Did you see anyone?"

Gabe rubbed the back of his neck, scowling. "No. They smashed a window in your bedroom. That's how they got in."

"Ma'am," the officer said, "from the looks of things, I'd say it was a crime of opportunity. Empty house, kids breaking a window, searching for stuff they could steal and sell quickly on the street."

I frowned. The TV was still in the living room, as was my computer. If they were looking for quick money, wouldn't those things be the first to go? I glanced at Gabe to see if he was thinking the same thing, but he just shrugged. "I can't tell what's missing," he said. "If anything."

Great.

"If either of you can think of anyone suspicious who's been hanging around the neighborhood lately, please let us know. We'll check them out," the officer said, putting his tiny notebook back in his pocket.

Before I could stop myself, I blurted out, "Elijah Harris."

Gabe's gaze snapped to mine. He didn't look happy I'd mentioned it, but I didn't give a shit. It was my house that had been broken into, my life tossed and turned over like nothing but trash. My best friend who was dead.

The officer pulled his notepad out again. "Can you say that once more, ma'am?"

I did, then gave him the story. "He showed up here yesterday, and he seemed pissed off. I think he had something to do with Alexis Barnes's murder too," I added, then swallowed hard, my heart hammering against my rib cage. "She came here to Harpers Ferry to try and get away from him, but somehow he tracked her down."

Gabe was wearing that stoic soldier expression he got when things were difficult, I noticed. I could tell he was upset, though, by that tiny muscle twitching near his tense jaw. Maybe I shouldn't have said anything, but dammit, I was scared.

"Right," the officer said, scribbling notes on his pad before closing it again. He sighed, then gave me a patronizing look. "I'll give that name to the detective working on the case."

I'd seen that look before, too many times. They wouldn't do anything.

Fuck.

"Thanks, officer," Gabe said, jumping in again. "Can you keep us updated? Let us know if you find out who did this?"

"Yep." The officer started down the stairs to the sidewalk, then looked back at us. "Break-ins happen, though, folks. In fact, the trend is on the rise here in Jefferson County. Can't guarantee anything."

"I know," Gabe said, smiling politely. "But still. Keep us in the loop, if you can. Thanks again."

I stood there on the porch, seething inside, as the officer got into his car and pulled away.

EIGHT

I hated that this had happened on my watch. Hated even more the look on Charlotte's face. Fuck. It felt like I'd betrayed her, or at least my vow to keep her and Savannah safe. Cursing under my breath, I walked inside and stood amid the mess.

As bad as it looked from the front door, she hadn't seen the worst of it yet. Her bedroom was demolished, like whoever broke in had a personal vendetta against her. The pillows and mattress were sliced and the stuffing strewn everywhere. Bottles had been shattered and their contents smeared or splashed on the walls. Floorboards pried up. Even what looked to be fist marks smashed into the drywall.

About the only corner not touched was where Savannah's pack and play was. That had immediately made me think about Alexis's abusive ex, the guy claiming to be Savannah's father.

Yeah. This felt personal. Whoever did this had been full of rage.

About the only positive thing I could say was that nothing of value seemed to be gone. All the electronics and jewelry and other items that could've been sold off for cash were untouched. But knowing the perpetrator hadn't taken anything important didn't make me feel better. Just the opposite, in fact. I steeled my resolve to catch the fucker responsible and make sure they paid.

When I'd shown the police officer Charlotte's bedroom, he had zeroed in on the smashed window and the fist marks in the walls, but it wasn't like he had a CSI team he could call to sweep the place. Small towns like Harpers Ferry didn't have the budget for all that lab stuff, especially for a routine break-in. And as far as he was concerned, that's what this was. That much was clear from his reaction.

But my gut told me this was something more. As I stood in what looked like the aftermath of a tornado, I reached into my pocket and pulled out the pacifier I'd found lying on the floor under the window during my initial search.

It was shiny and new, not worn and half gummed to death like Savannah's other ones. She was teething and, I'd quickly learned, would gnaw on anything she could get in her mouth, including herself and other people. A "gift" left for the baby only reinforced the most obvious suspect: Elijah Harris. If he'd done this, that meant he was coming after Charlotte now, and holy fuck. I squeezed the pacifier tight in my fist.

She'd brought his name up to the police, then cut me a look like I'd be upset about it. I wasn't pissed, truthfully, though I wasn't sure it would do much good. After all, Harris had been wearing a West Virginia State Police uniform when he'd come here that day to talk to Charlotte, and everyone knew that law enforcement guys took care of their own. I understood the sentiment. We did the same in the SEALs.

Except when one of our own was rotten to the core. In that case, we normally dealt with it internally. The Navy had military courts set up for just such situations.

But we weren't in the military now, and this evil bastard wanted to take Savannah from me. I couldn't let that happen. I wouldn't let that happen. The pacifier squeaked as I crushed it in my hand, and I shoved it back into my pocket, then walked down the hall to the living room.

Charlotte had cleared a spot on the couch and taken a seat, cooing to Savannah to keep her calm. Even though she was making nonsense noises for the baby, her face looked the way it had the night Elijah Harris had shown up on her doorstep.

Terrified.

How the fuck could I let this happen on my watch?

I didn't want to tell her about her bedroom, but I had to. She deserved to know. I pulled out the pacifier and handed it to her. "Found this in your room. Is it Savannah's?"

She shook her head, the color draining from her face. "No."

"Didn't think so." I scrubbed a hand over my face before continuing, rushing the words out before I couldn't say them anymore. "If this is Harris, we can't trust the cops to handle it. This, combined with the fact that nothing's missing, tells me it's personal. Until I can get a handle on Harris and what he's up to, I think we need to lay low for a couple of days." I took a deep breath, wanting to tell Charlotte it would all be okay but knowing I couldn't. Not yet. Maybe not ever. *Concentrate.* I cleared my throat, staring the wall instead of her because it was easier. "Can you get someone to cover your shifts at the tavern?"

Charlotte didn't say anything. She gave a slow nod, like she wasn't taking it all in yet.

"Good. I don't want you going anywhere alone right now." I headed for the door, needing time and space and fresh air to keep from putting my own fist through a wall in frustration. "I'm going to walk the perimeter again. Make sure the officer didn't miss anything."

I knew Gabe was right: lying low for the time being was a good idea. That didn't keep me from feeling trapped in my own house after two days, though. Not that I didn't have enough to keep me busy there.

Between getting all-new housewares delivered—up to and including a new mattress and bedding—and having a handyman come to repair the damage to my bedroom walls and then another gal in to paint them, it was a lot to deal with. Those delivery people had to be getting sick of seeing my face. And I didn't like thinking about the cost of replacing all that stuff.

Even so, I felt like didn't know what to do with myself during the brief downtimes. I was used to the constant go, go, go of working at the tavern—and, apart from work, to doing what I wanted when I wanted. But none of that was possible right now. Not with Elijah Harris out there somewhere. I called in, sure, but my staff at the bar were too good at their jobs. Turned out they didn't need me as much as I needed them, dammit.

I never really knew what being cooped up meant until now.

"Come on." Gabe stepped in front of me to stop my pacing. "Let's take a walk. The air will do us good."

Walking for pleasure wasn't something I often did. No time. But now all I had was time, and staying cooped up inside sure wasn't helping my mental state. Maybe getting out for a little while would help. "Okay."

We got Savannah ready and started walking down the block toward the trail to the river. When I'd first moved into my house, I used to come down here sometimes on Sundays. It was pretty and peaceful. Savannah was content in her stroller, as usual, and even though the day was a bit overcast, the air was still warm. The river was beautiful, too, clear and sparkling. We stopped a moment to look at it, and that's when I noticed the funny look on Gabe's face. Not sad, exactly, but close to it.

"What's wrong?" I asked.

"What?" He glanced over at me, like he was just then realizing I was there. "Oh, nothing. I'm fine."

I narrowed my eyes at him. "You don't look fine. You look upset."

He shrugged.

Then it hit me. He'd been gone for ages, and being here must be triggering all sorts of memories. Good and bad.

"I'm sorry." Without thinking, I reached over and put my hand on his arm. "It must be hard for you, being back here where your family was. Seeing these places again, remembering how things used to be."

He shrugged again, then stayed quiet for so long I thought he might not answer. Finally, staring out at the river, he said, "It was hard, at first. But it's not so bad today. I don't have that sinking feeling in my chest, like there's a black hole there or something."

"Well, that's a start."

We walked on, stopping halfway across the bridge to stare down into the water.

Gabe sighed, then looked over at me. "It's getting easier. Did I tell you I ran into Mrs. Kepner the other day when I went to get my bloodwork done?"

"I haven't thought about her in forever! How is she?"

"Fine, I guess. Maybe a bit lonely? She asked me to write to her." He shook his head and looked away. "Guess I'll need to get better at that once I'm back with my team."

"Right."

I knew he'd be leaving once this whole mess was over, but hearing it felt like an electric shock, jarring and uncomfortable. Truth was, I'd gotten used to having Gabe around, even though it had only been a little over a week.

It was nice, knowing I could depend on him. I wasn't used to that from a man. My dad left—for the last time—when I was seven. Now, I doubted I could make the whole stable relationship thing work with anyone, even someone who seemed as wonderful as Gabe. Not that I was considering anything with him. So I did what I always did. Sucked it up and stuffed my emotions down deep. "When do you have to go back?"

"Not sure yet." He rested his elbows on the railing and clasped his hands, head lowered. "My CO is doing everything he can to keep me here until the paternity test results come back and they hold the custody hearing. I have sixty leave days banked, so hopefully that will be enough." He sighed. "I wish I didn't have to leave the rest of my team in the lurch like this, but I know they'll understand."

"Sounds like you guys are close," I said. Then, after a brief hesitation, I added, "Like a family."

He gave a curt nod in response, that stoic shield dropping back into place, letting me know I'd gotten too close.

We started back toward the house, and despite Gabe shutting me out at the end there, our walk did make me feel better. The combination of fresh air, cooing baby, and strong, silent bodyguard helped.

Once we got home, after Gabe did a walk-through to make sure the house was safe while I put Savannah down for a nap. When I walked back into the family room, he was staring out the window like he was doing surveillance.

"Hey, thanks for taking me outside. I feel a lot better now."

"You're welcome," he answered. "Getting outside always helps me clear my mind too."

I was reminded of everything he'd admitted during the walk. He'd closed up when I pushed beyond his comfort zone, but I wasn't about to let it go. "You know, you can always talk to me when you feel like the black hole is coming back. I'm a good listener."

I'd walked up behind him, and he spun around as if startled. We were just a few inches apart, closer than we'd ever been.

We stood there, and it felt like there was some invisible cord tying us together, keeping us from moving, from talking, from breathing. His gaze flicked from my eyes down to my lips, then back again, and a sudden burst of warmth ignited inside me like fireworks.

This close, I could see the hint of dark stubble along the skin of his tight jaw, hear the catch of his breath, feel the heat of him surrounding me, drawing me closer. Even afterward, I couldn't say which one of us moved first. All I knew was that one second we were looking at each other, and the next we were kissing.

His strong arms wrapped around my waist, pulling me closer. I placed my hands against his chest to brace myself as his lips found mine, shocked that it was happening and dizzy from the sensations. Gabe wasn't tentative. He seemed to want the kiss as much as I did, and when I arched into him, pressing my breasts against his chest, he made a gruff noise.

Which is why it made no sense when he broke the kiss and moved away from me.

And damn. If I'd felt awkward before, it was nothing compared to now.

What. The. Hell. Had I been thinking?

I hadn't been. And neither had he, that much was clear by the way he strode out of the room without even looking at me.

How were we going to play this off? Pretend it hadn't happened? I couldn't imagine that would be possible, considering the fact that my lips were still tingling from his, and I could still taste him.

Worse yet, I wanted to do it again.

NINE

I woke up the next morning at eight. Eight a.m. I couldn't tell you the last time that happened. At first I panicked, thinking I was late to the bar and I'd miss the delivery guy with the early supplies and then I'd be short for the weekend. But then I remembered I was staying home, with Gabe and Savannah, and I relaxed a bit, staring at the ceiling. It was nice, I realized, having them here. The house didn't seem quite so big or cold with other heartbeats down the hallway.

Finally, after a yawn and a stretch, I slipped on my robe, used the bathroom, and headed for the kitchen as happy baby squeals echoed down the hall. I couldn't help smiling myself in response.

I found Gabe sitting at the table trying to feed Savannah. It looked like there was more banana puree on him than in her mouth, but I had to give him credit for trying.

"Morning," I said as naturally as I could, considering I couldn't stop thinking about our kiss.

"Hey," he said, focused solely on Savannah.

I poured myself a cup of coffee and tried not to laugh as Gabe negotiated with the baby.

"Come on, little girl," he pleaded. "You've only got a few more mouthfuls to go. And it's so good." I pretended not to watch as he slurped the spoon. "See? Yummy!"

Savannah giggled. I turned just in time to see Gabe bring a heaping spoonful of puree toward her, only to have Savannah laugh and smack it away, sending it splattering all over him.

"Seriously?" he asked. "You're really going to act like that?"

She seemed to enjoy his displeasure and giggled harder, until his frown cracked and he joined in.

"Welcome to my world." I laughed with them. "Doesn't look like I need to ask how it's going. I'm pretty sure there's more food stuck to the two of you than in her stomach."

Gabe gave me a look, banana puree crusted on his face, and Savannah burbled happily. "You're not helping."

"I wasn't trying to." I smirked, enjoying my smart-assery a moment—plus the fact that it was someone besides me getting pummeled in the face with banana mush—before I took pity on him and walked over to help.

"Here, let me help." I grabbed some baby wipes from the container at the center of the table and cleaned Savannah up while Gabe wiped his own face. "I'll get her changed and set up in her playpen if you clean up in here."

"Deal," he said, looking down at his ruined T-shirt.

Once Savannah was happily playing with her giraffe toy, I headed back to the kitchen, only to stop in my tracks when I saw Gabe standing at the sink rinsing dishes. I had to admire the view for a second. *How* had I missed that ass?

The muscles of his strong back rippled beneath his white T-shirt, reminding me of how those same muscles had felt beneath my hands the day before when we'd kissed—and whoops. No. Nope. Not going there. Because wanting him that way was far too slippery a slope, and if I started thinking about that, then I'd start wondering what he looked like with the T-shirt off altogether, and that would lead to what he'd look like completely naked, and...

My gaze trailed up his body, taking in every detail like I needed to memorize him. My breath came quicker, and I felt myself getting hot and bothered, filled with visions of what I could do to him. With him. What I *wanted* to do with him.

When he turned around and met my gaze, I jumped and coughed, trying to play off the fact that he'd caught me fantasizing about him. Between my awkwardness and my red-hot face, it was pretty obvious what had been going through my head.

Gabe looked away quickly. Yup, he knew, and that made it awkward, because now we both had to pretend like it didn't happen.

Part of me knew it was for the best. We had no business getting involved like that. He'd be leaving as soon as this whole mess with Savannah was taken care of, and I had my hands full with the bar to run and now a baby to raise, so forgetting about it was the best thing for all of us.

So why did I feel so disappointed when he stormed off, like something precious and rare between us had been lost?

Worse, why did it scare me right down to my soul?

Shit.

I tossed the washcloth I'd been using into the sink, then walked into the living room. Retreat wasn't my usual MO, but sometimes you had to get away from a situation in order to figure out the best way forward. And frankly, I couldn't think straight with Charlotte so close, looking at me like she wanted to gobble me up whole one second, her expression turning petrified the next.

It was confusing as hell, and I didn't like it one bit.

Until I'd returned to Harpers Ferry, my life had been neat and orderly, following a predictable course that I was comfortable with. Now, though, that had all been shot to shit. I scrubbed a hand over my face, wrinkling my nose at the lingering smell of bananas on my skin, far more aware of the weight of Charlotte's stare still tingling on the back of my neck than I should have been. I didn't want to think about that kiss.

It had already taken up way more of my time and my brain than it should. I'd tossed and turned most of the night thinking about it, imagining what would've happened if we hadn't stopped when we did, if I'd carried her to her bedroom, stripped her bare, then made love to every delectable inch of her…

Fuck.

Truth was, that kiss had been good. Better than good. Great.

Amazing.

But that didn't make it right. I should've known better. Should've kept my lips to myself and not complicated things between us any more than they already were. Didn't matter that she kissed me back like she was desperate for it too. Or that she felt like she belonged in my arms. None of that would help us at all.

I'd be leaving as soon as I got things with my daughter sorted out. Charlotte could remain as involved as she wanted in Savannah's life, and she could also get on with running her business and creating a future for herself independent of me.

Never mind that all I wanted to do was walk over and kiss her again. It couldn't happen.

Except then it did.

I wasn't even sure how I ended up back in the kitchen standing in front of Charlotte, who was looking up at me with her big, hazel eyes wide with wonder, but then she was in my arms and my mouth was on hers and it was even better than I remembered.

This time it was longer and deeper and so much hotter. She gasped and clung to me like she'd never let me go, and I swept my tongue into her mouth, tasting her again. Coffee this time. Still sweet as pie. I felt like I was drowning, but I couldn't get enough. Charlotte had always been tough, even back in high school.

But staying with her now, I'd seen her softer side. The way she cared for Savannah, and the kindness she'd shown me the day we walked on the trail. She might be fierce on the outside, but she had a nurturing heart.

I pulled her closer, and she looped her leg around my waist, her robe parting so our bodies were pressed together. I growled low in my throat, and she groaned, both of us clinging and clawing and trying to get more.

Carefully, I turned and lifted her to sit on the edge of the counter, then spread her legs, moving between them and grinding against the heat of her body, letting her know in no uncertain terms how badly I wanted her. My cock ached, threatening to burst through the fly of my jeans. I would've taken her then, but a squeak from the living room had us pulling apart fast.

The sounds of our breathing filled the kitchen as we rested our foreheads together. I was panting, and I could feel Charlotte trembling against me. My blood sang in my veins, urging me to touch her, to bring her back into the moment we'd been about to share. But no. We had more than ourselves to think about. We had Savannah.

Finally, Charlotte tightened the belt on her robe, then hopped down, her body brushing mine and making me bite back another groan full of want. "Let me just check on her."

I watched her walk to the living room and pick up the baby, knowing it was for the best. We had no business touching each other, wanting each other like that. And yet I did. Maybe it had been too long since I'd been with a woman.

Or maybe it was simply Charlotte, being wonderful.

"She okay?" I managed to force out, the words sounding rough and wrecked to my own ears. "Does she need to be changed? I can do it."

God. A month ago I'd never have believed you if you'd told me I'd be standing here offering to diaper a kid. Hell, a month ago I wouldn't have known how. But now everything was different. Because of the woman in front of me and the baby in her arms. I wasn't sure how I felt about that.

I'd always prided myself on my ability to adapt. It was one of my greatest assets as a SEAL. Sure, our team planned ahead of time for our missions, but unexpected things always happened in the field. Curve balls. Well, life had thrown me one huge fucking curve ball now, and I was completely mystified as to how to handle it.

Think, dude. Think.

Except I couldn't think clearly or rationally about any of this, because my emotions were involved now. We hadn't yet gotten the results from my blood test, but I knew in my heart that Savannah was mine.

She looked like me, smiled like me. She even laughed like me. There was no doubt she was mine.

And where did that leave Charlotte? She obviously loved Savannah as much as I did. How would we handle things once the custody case was settled? An unwanted memory of Elijah Harris and his claim rushed back to my mind, and my hackles went up. Guard-dog mode activated. No way did I want that guy anywhere near either of my girls.

My girls?

The possessive streak inside me knocked me off my feet.

Finding myself in the living room again, with no idea how I'd gotten there from the kitchen, I sank down on the sofa and raked my hands through my hair. Since when had I started thinking of them as my girls? Probably about when I'd kissed Charlotte the first time. Or maybe it had been after the break-in. Or maybe the day Harris showed up on Charlotte's doorstep.

Fuck. I didn't know when it had started. All I knew for certain was that this was all getting out of control, and I needed to stop it. We had to keep our heads on straight to get through what was ahead with Harris.

But I also knew that at some point we'd have to revisit this issue, no matter how awkward it was or how much both of us wanted to avoid it. Because if life had taught me anything, it was that ignoring shit and hoping it would go away on its own never worked.

That was why I'd come back here in the first place, after all. To deal with all the stuff with my family that I'd tried to wish away but that still roiled beneath the surface. The last thing I wanted was to do the same with this thing between me and Charlotte. We had Savannah to think about now. We couldn't mess this up.

Which meant we'd talk about it again, sooner rather than later. Just not right now.

Because right now, I needed to get myself together before I did something stupid, like kiss her again and never let her go.

TEN

Charlotte took Savannah into her room to give her a bath, since the baby wipes only went so far in removing that pureed banana smell, and I went back to the kitchen to clean up and get myself back under control. My blood was still slamming through my veins, and my heart felt like a jackhammer in my chest. All over a kiss.

A kiss that could've turned into much, much more...

"Hey, Gabe?" Charlotte called from down the hall.

"Yeah," I said, the word emerging a lot rougher than I wanted. I cleared my throat and tried again. "Yes?"

"I think we need to go back to Alexis's house and get the rest of Savannah's things," she said. "The baby's been wearing the same couple of outfits I grabbed that first day, and she needs more. Plus, I want to get more of her toys, so she stays happy and doesn't get bored."

"Okay." I scrubbed down the table, hoping the manual labor would get my still-hard cock to calm down. Maybe an errand and some fresh air was just what I needed. "We can go after you finish giving Savannah her bath, if you want."

"Sounds good. I'll call my mom and see if she can watch the baby," Charlotte called back. "I know it sounds silly, but I don't want Savannah to see the house. Not with everything that happened."

"Good plan." It didn't sound silly to me. Not really. I wanted to spare my daughter all the heartache and pain in life, no matter how young she was and whether or not she'd remember.

After I got the kitchen scrubbed clean and myself presentable again, Charlotte and I dropped the baby off at her mom's—with a warning not to open the door to anyone but us—and set off for Alexis's house.

We parked at the curb and got out. The crime scene tape was gone from the door, which meant the police department was through gathering evidence. Normally, they'd turn the property back over to the family afterward, but since Alexis didn't have anyone, I assumed the bank would probably take it back. That thought bothered me more than I wanted to admit. Not the bank, but Alexis being alone. We'd only had the one night together, but still.

Charlotte pulled out her key and let us in. That surprised me.

"What?" Charlotte asked over her shoulder.

"Well, unless they broke a window to get inside, like what happened at your house, the front door is the obvious entry point. But from what I can see, the door's fine and the locks are the same, since your key worked."

She frowned. "And?"

"And that means Alexis probably knew her assailant and let them in."

"Oh." Charlotte shuddered. "Right. Let's get this done as quickly as possible. Being here creeps me out."

"Don't touch anything you don't have to," I said, closing the door behind us with my hip. "Just pack what you want of Savannah's stuff. I'm going to take a look around while you do that and see if there's anything left behind the police might have missed."

She went off to the nursery, and I started scanning the area. I didn't see any signs of forced entry. No busted windows or smashed-in doors. So the assailant must've left the same way they'd come in, through the front door.

Once I'd cleared the living room and kitchen, I headed down the hall to the master bedroom. Covering my hand with the hem of my T-shirt, I opened the drawers, then rooted around inside. Nothing out of the ordinary at all, until I opened the nightstand drawer. It seemed to stick a bit, and I wiggled it around until it slid out completely. Wedged between the drawer and the back was a small journal.

Bingo.

I pulled it out and flipped through it, seeing a blur of entries and some photos stuck in between the pages. I shoved it in my jacket pocket, then replaced the drawer. The book might not give us any useful information, but whatever was in there, Alexis had wanted to keep it hidden.

My stomach twisted as I did a quick search of the rest of the rooms before meeting Charlotte back near the front door. After we loaded all the baby stuff into the back of the car, I handed her the journal. "Found this in Alexis's bedroom," I told her. "If you want, I'll drive so you can look at it on the way."

Charlotte flipped through the journal as we headed back to her house, her expression growing sadder the longer she read. "Wow. I had no idea how much she'd suffered. We were best friends, but she never told me some of this stuff. The abuse." She showed me an entry. "This last entry here is from a few days before she died. She says that Elijah made a new Facebook account and messaged her. She didn't reply, but he told her how sorry he was for all the pain he'd caused her and for what he'd put her through. He said he just wanted her and the baby to be a family."

"Asshole." I gripped the steering wheel harder than necessary. "That's what abusers always say, to lure their target out." Then the words registered, and my heart dropped. "Wait a minute. I thought you said that Alexis didn't tell Elijah about the baby."

"She didn't," Charlotte said, her face pale. "She said she'd left without telling him. So how'd he find out?"

We stopped for a red light, and I took a deep breath and tried to think about it objectively. "Honestly, it probably wouldn't be that hard to find out. If he had another fake account on Facebook and sent her a friend request, and she accepted not knowing it was him, he could see all the stuff she posted. Did she ever share photos of Savannah?"

Charlotte swallowed hard, her eyes huge. "Oh God. Yes, she did. She loved taking pictures of the baby."

"That's probably it, then." The light turned green, and I accelerated, raking one hand through my hair, forcing myself to breathe to help dissipate the growing anger and anxiety inside me. The thought of Elijah Harris stalking an innocent woman and her child—my child— online made me want to hurt something. Mainly him. "He must've checked in on Alexis at some point. Might've been months after she left him, when he finally started to care about her again. If he saw Savannah on her profile, that could've been the impetus for him to start digging around to find their address. Between social media and the resources he'd have through the police, it wouldn't have taken him long to track them down."

"Jesus." Charlotte closed the journal with trembling hands. "That's awful."

Awful didn't begin to cover it.

After stopping to pick up the baby, we went back to Charlotte's house. She took Savannah back to her room to get her settled in for a nap while I unloaded the stuff from the car. Then I went to the guest room to make a call. Elijah Harris wasn't the only one with contacts.

I must've caught my CO before he went to bed this time, because he answered on the first ring. I gave him a quick rundown of the situation and the journal I'd found, then asked him what he thought. I needed perspective. I was too close to be objective, even though my instincts were telling me I was right. Elijah Harris was behind all this.

Smith, my CO, agreed—to some extent. "There could be other viable explanations, or other people involved, but I do think Harris is at least involved. It would be too much of a coincidence if he wasn't. What I do know for sure is that that journal and any other evidence you have needs to go to the police."

I sighed and sank down onto the edge of the bed. "I know. I guess I was hoping to find some answers myself before I gave it to them."

"You know," Smith said, "Ryeland just opened his security firm in DC."

"Really?" I looked up then. Matt Ryeland had retired from our SEAL team a while back. He was a good guy. Trustworthy.

"Yeah. Maybe you should get ahold of him and have him help you do a little digging into this Elijah Harris guy. See if you can put him in Harpers Ferry on the night of the murder."

"Okay. I will. Thanks, sir." I sat back and rubbed my eyes. "Any word on my extended leave yet?"

"I'm working on it right now, actually." Smith's voice rang with the self-confidence that seemed a natural part of him. "The rest of the team is still willing to donate leave, if it comes to that, but we'll see what the brass says first. Don't worry about it. You're covered either way. We've got your back."

"Thank you." The stress of this situation was exhausting, and it was nice to hear that at least there was one piece of it I didn't need to worry about. I started to end the call, but Smith stopped me.

"Have you been to the cemetery yet?" he asked.

Fuck.

"No." I squeezed my eyes shut. "With everything else going on, I haven't had time to even think about it yet." Not a total lie. I had been busy. "But I'll go, as soon as I get a chance."

"Hmm." Smith sounded skeptical. I couldn't blame him. "You're full of shit, son. Seriously, go. It'll be good for you, I promise."

"I will."

We'd just finished the call when Charlotte knocked on the doorframe and stuck her head into the guest room. "Savannah's out like a light," she said, smiling. "Being with my mom wore her out, I think."

"Having met your mom, that's understandable," I joked, even though I wasn't quite feeling like laughing right then.

"Mind if I come in?" she asked.

"Sure," I said. "It's your house."

She sat down beside me on the bed, and I caught the faintest hint of vanilla. It made me want to lean closer and drink her in, but I forced myself to keep my distance.

"What are we going to do now?" she asked.

I told her about my conversation with my CO and his suggestion to contact Matt. "I think he could help us dig up more information on Harris. I really think we need to connect him to the night of Alexis's murder before we go to the cops. Otherwise, seeing as he's law enforcement, they might not take us seriously. We need all the pieces to fall into place before we make our case to them."

"Agreed. We need everything to be airtight." She sighed. "Let's make the call."

I saw the strain on her face. She was doing her best to keep it together, but there was no hiding the haunted look in her eyes. A murder, a baby, a forced entry, and what amounted to a stranger living under the same roof would probably break the average woman, but there was nothing average about Charlotte. Hell, she could probably run boot camp.

Which is why I found it so strange that my protective instinct went into overdrive every time she was near me.

ELEVEN

I thought she'd scurry away after cementing our plan, but Charlotte never ceased to surprise me. Her tentative perch on the edge of the bed slowly shifted until she was curled up like a cat. I wanted to reach out and pet her, but I knew I shouldn't.

It felt so easy, talking with her. She caught me up on the town gossip, and before long we were laughing like we didn't have a care in the world. The tension in my shoulders eased a notch every time she smiled at me. We were... *bantering*. Like we were on a date, even though we both knew how far from the truth that was.

"So," I said, taking off my boots before stretching out my legs on the bed, my back against the headboard, "what's a nice girl like you still doing on the market?" I gave her a quick smile. "I mean, not that there's anything wrong with that. I just..."

She laughed. "It's fine. Honestly, I haven't had time for romance. I figure I'll focus on that later, after the tavern's more profitable."

"Hmm." As someone who'd avoided getting tied down for years, I knew the lie when I heard it. Still, it wasn't my place to push, so I didn't. We sat a while in silence before she continued.

"I don't know," Charlotte said, running her hand along the comforter and avoiding my gaze, a slight frown knitting her dark brows together. "Sometimes I think my dad screwed me up pretty bad."

My chest ached at her words. Harpers Ferry was a small town, so I'd grown up knowing about her family situation. Now, in the soft glow of the lamplight, we were being real with one another.

She shrugged, her frown deepening. "I mean, without him around, I never really had a good role model for that stuff, you know? The one time I did fall in love with somebody, it didn't work out so well. He ended up moving to England, and I stayed here. Since then, I haven't put too much effort into it, I guess."

I nodded, exhaling slowly, staring down at my hands in my lap. It wasn't like I was some kind of relationship expert either, seeing as how avoidance was my main MO.

"What about you?" she asked, scooting down to lay her head on the pillow, glancing up at me through her lashes. Fuck, why did she have to be so irresistible? I wanted to cup her cheek, run my fingers through her tousled hair—but I didn't. Because if she gave me that look... the one that told me to keep going... I'd drop my mouth toward hers, ever so slowly, until our lips touched. Her arms would circle my neck and pull me down on top of her, and I'd...

"Gabe, are you okay?"

I coughed and shifted to cover my crotch, startled out of my pornographic daydream. "Yep, fine."

"I asked about your love life. Or are you going to dodge the question?"

I felt like I owed her an explanation, after she'd been so open with me.

"It's hard to have anything too serious with someone when you're always on the move." I took a deep breath. "And… after I lost my family in the accident, my SEAL team became like a surrogate one. But that's risky too."

"How so?" That frown was back on her lovely face. I longed to trace the furrow between her brows to soothe it.

I lifted a shoulder. "Those guys are like brothers to me, but I could lose any of them at any time on a mission. The places we go, they're dangerous. It's why we're there. To defuse the conflicts no one else can. To handle the situation, however we need to. Sometimes people get hurt. Sometimes worse. So, no matter how close you get, you still subconsciously hold a bit back to protect yourself, in case the worst happens." I shook my head and stared up at the ceiling. "Or maybe that's just me. Afraid to lose more people I care about."

"Oh, Gabe." She reached over and took my hand.

We sat there for a while, not saying anything. The feeling of her soft hand on top of mine soothed me.

Finally, I looked over at her, and she'd fallen asleep. For the best, I supposed, since I really didn't want to talk about my feelings anymore. It was hard, and now they felt all knotted and thorny inside me. Uncomfortable. Inviting as it looked to curl up beside her and take a snooze myself, I was too restless to nap.

Besides, I had an important phone call to make.

I slipped out of the room and dialed Matt Ryeland.

"Ryeland Security."

"Hey, dude. It's Gabe Kelley."

"Gabe, my man!" Matt laughed. "It's been a minute. What's going on?"

"I'm taking some leave right now. Dealing with some family stuff here in Harpers Ferry," I said. "So, has working security dulled your senses yet?"

Matt snorted. "Like hell. Once a SEAL, always a SEAL, my man. Nothing's dulling those instincts, whether you're wearing the uniform or not." We chitchatted a bit, and then Matt said, "So, to what do I owe this call? Since you've never been one for hanging out and being sociable for the heck of it."

"Actually, I wondered if you could run a background check for me," I said, cringing that he'd called me on my loner tendencies. It wasn't that I didn't like hanging out with my friends. I was just usually dealing with fifty things at once. I liked keeping busy, liked to keep moving. It kept the ghosts at bay. Or at least it had—until I'd come home and stopped running. Now the ghosts were permanent fixtures, and I was learning to live with that.

He scoffed. "Seriously? Uh, yeah. Background checks are like Security 101. Child's play. Happy to run one for you. Have to say I'm a little disappointed, though. Here I thought you'd give me a real challenge. Like some paramilitary espionage shit."

"Oh, it's gonna be a challenge, all right," I replied as I pictured the man trying to take my child away from me. "Listen, this one's kind of sensitive. He's a state trooper. He's based out of DC or Virginia, not sure which. Name's Elijah Harris, and I need to know everything you can find out about him, particularly around September 23. Where he was, who he was with, what he ate, when he took a shit. Everything. Nothing's too trivial. Understood?"

"Got it," Matt said. "Challenge accepted. And sensitive is my middle name."

I laughed. "Wait. I thought it was 'dumbass.'"

"Only that one time in Hong Kong." He chuckled. "I'll get on this and get back to you as soon as I can."

"Thanks. I appreciate it."

We ended the call, and I walked into the kitchen. All I could do now was wait.

I grabbed a beer and settled in front of the TV, flipping channels and trying not to think about the challenges in front of me. Prioritizing what needed to happen next always helped center me, so I focused on the immediate: dinner. I was starving.

Charlotte padded down the hall looking adorably rumpled, cooing to Savannah. "She's hungry," she said, bouncing the baby in her arms.

"She's not the only one," I replied. "After you feed her, do you want to grab dinner in town? I was thinking we could hit the Coffee Mill."

"Sure," Charlotte said, smiling at me over her shoulder as she stood at the microwave. "I haven't been there in a while." She yawned. "Sorry I fell asleep on you. Guess I'm more tired than I thought."

"No problem. I took care of some stuff, so it's all good. I talked to my friend, and he's going to run the background check for us."

"Awesome." The microwave beeped, and she pulled the bottle out, checking the temp on her wrist before taking a seat at the table to feed the baby. "How long will it take?"

"Not sure. Probably a couple of days, I think."

Once Savannah finished her bottle, we put her in her stroller and started walking toward the diner. It wasn't far, and the weather was still nice, not too chilly. As we neared downtown, though, I started regretting my decision.

Inside a car, it was easier to not think about my past, my family—to keep the nostalgia at bay and compartmentalize things. But walking, bumping into folks I hadn't seen in ages, brought back memories of the last time I'd been here with my family.

There was the arcade, where Isaac and I had fought about that stupid pinball machine and who'd play first. It seemed so ridiculous now, but I remembered being super pissed at my younger brother, even though now I could see that he'd simply wanted to impress me and show off his skills. He'd wanted me to think he was cool.

God, I missed him.

"Hey," Charlotte said, nudging me with her shoulder, her expression concerned. "You okay?"

"Fine," I said. I was good at covering shit up after all this time.

"Liar."

At least I *thought* I was good at it.

"Seriously," Charlotte said, glancing at me out of the corner of her eye. "I can tell when something's bothering you. You get all quiet and twitchy."

"I do not twitch." My flat stare did little to dim her bright smile. Okay. Maybe I twitched now and then when I was tense. Whatever. She kept watching me, and finally I caved. I shook my head. "It's nothing. I just…" Deep breath. "It's the ten-year anniversary of my family's deaths. My original plan was to come home to go to the cemetery and see their graves. I've never been since the funeral." My shrug felt sheepish. "I'm still trying to build up my courage and all, I guess. It's hard."

I hated how weak that sounded, but then Charlotte's hand was on my arm and she was giving me one of those soft looks, and I sort of melted inside. "Gabe, I'm so sorry. Would it help if I went with you?"

A lump formed in my throat, and I swallowed hard around it. God. What the hell was wrong with me? I was never like this. I always kept my emotions stuffed down deep. But somehow Charlotte cracked me wide open, with her big, beautiful eyes and sincere heart. I coughed to cover the inappropriate need swelling inside me to pull her into my arms and never let her go. "Uh, no. Thanks, but I need to do this on my own."

Charlotte's hand dropped away, and I missed her touch immediately.

The diner was relatively empty, which was good because I didn't feel like playing catch-up with anyone else. The waitress seated us in a corner booth, and Charlotte busied herself with the menu and the baby.

Damn it, she was right: I was twitching. I couldn't get comfortable on the padded bench, and the words on the menu seemed too small to read, even though my vision was perfect. It felt like Charlotte was plotting something, readying herself for battle by ignoring me.

"How about if we go tomorrow?"

And there it was. Her opening shot.

I started to object, but she held up a hand, cutting me off. "Hear me out. The baby and I can sit in the car while you go to their graves. That way you're alone, but not alone."

I wanted to say no. I wanted to stand firm behind my decision to do this by myself. But damn.

She was right. And having them in the car wouldn't stop me from doing what I needed to do out there. If the tears came, she wouldn't see them. Plus, I could keep an eye on her and the baby, in case Harris tried to pull some more shit.

It wasn't a big deal, but it kind of felt like it was.

Finally, I gave a curt nod. "Fine. Tomorrow, then."

TWELVE

The next day, I was second-guessing my decision to let Charlotte and Savannah go with me. What if I couldn't get my shit together by the time I walked back to the car? Or, worse, what if I stood at my family's graves and felt nothing at all? No closure, nothing. Bringing Charlotte and the baby seemed like a bad idea all around, but I'd made the commitment and I'd follow through on it. As I got ready that morning, I tried to clear my mind.

I'd never planned to come back to Harpers Ferry again anyway, let alone for something like this. Ten years. A decade my family had been gone and I'd been an orphan. Hell of an anniversary.

I'd never been an anxious person, but it was hitting me hard today. I was moody and couldn't seem to stand still. Once I was dressed, I went out to the kitchen, where Charlotte was feeding Savannah.

Normally, the baby relaxed me, so I picked her up from her jumper to kiss her and she started crying, apparently picking up on my swirling emotions. Guess that old wives' tale was correct, huh? Babies were psychic that way. Or else she was pissed about the jumper, because my girl really did love bouncing around in that thing.

Regardless, I was on edge.

On our way into town, we stopped at the local florist because Charlotte had insisted that we get a bouquet.

"It's tradition," she said as we walked inside. "What about this one?"

I wrinkled my nose at the pink and white carnations. "No. It looks wilted."

"It's not wilted," Charlotte said, giving me a look. "And keep your voice down. The owners might hear."

"Anything I can help with?" a woman behind the counter asked.

Before I could refuse, Charlotte stepped in and explained that we needed cemetery flowers. The owner led us over to a different section, and I ended up choosing a large arrangement of calla lilies. The owner wrapped them up for me, and we headed back to the car while I tried not to grip the flowers so hard I crushed them. It was a beautiful arrangement, and I wished I was going anywhere but where we were headed.

Except it was time. Time to stop running. Time to lay things to rest, literally.

What felt like a small eternity later, we got to the cemetery and wove through the maze of small lanes inside until we reached the section where my family was buried. It was near the back, in a quiet spot near some large oak trees. Picturesque. Calming. There was a bench and everything. I'd forgotten about that.

I parked, then sat there, like an idiot, trying to get my legs to move and my brain to calm.

"Are you sure you want us to stay in the car?" Charlotte asked while Savannah gurgled in her car seat in the back.

"Yes," I said, staring out the windshield, but I still made no move to leave. The sense of grief sat heavy on my chest, squeezing the air from my lungs. My body felt heavy, and my eyes stung.

I hung my head, whispering, "I don't know if I can do this."

Charlotte reached over and rubbed my back. "I'm here for you. Whatever you need from me. If you want me to go with you to their graves, I will."

I shook my head, but several more minutes passed before I opened the door. My movements felt odd, jerky, like I wasn't really in my body. Charlotte didn't say a word as she got out of the car and took Savannah out of the car seat. Suddenly, all I wanted was my daughter in my arms. That connection. That bond. As if she understood, Charlotte handed the baby to me. Savannah's small weight grounded me like nothing else.

I moved toward the plot slowly, the baby in one arm, the flowers tucked under the other, Charlotte waiting behind us. I kissed Savannah's cheek, inhaling her sweet baby smell, holding it inside me like a treasure.

"We're going to see your nan and pops and your Uncle Isaac," I said, my voice catching slightly and my vision blurring. I wanted her to know. Know them. Know where she came from. "You never got to meet them, baby girl, but they would've loved you so, so much. Same as I do." I told her about my parents and my brother, my tears flowing freely, but I didn't care.

At the grave site, I knelt and placed the flowers atop my parents' joint grave and dusted the leaves from the headstones. Then we took a seat on the bench nearby. There was a slight breeze, and the sky was overcast, but it wasn't raining or cold. Just quiet and peaceful. The pressure in my chest eased a bit. Savannah became fascinated with a squirrel nearby, and for the first time in a while, I smiled.

My family was gone, but I still felt them here. Still felt them all over this town. They were in me and always would be, no matter what. I sat there a while, taking it all in, and I realized Smith had been right. Coming here did help me, though there was still more I needed to do to be where I wanted emotionally.

Finally, after enough time had passed for me to work through some of my complicated emotions, I stood and walked back to the car. After another hug and kiss for my daughter, I handed her back to Charlotte, feeling about a hundred pounds lighter. "We can go now. What I need isn't here."

Charlotte watched me, tears in her own eyes despite her sunny smile.

Back at the house, I tried to keep the mood light. It was clear how much that visit to his families' graves had taken out of Gabe. Something major had shifted in him, and even though I could still see glimpses of grief in his eyes, he seemed more grounded.

Savannah was the perfect balm for his wrung-out heart. We sat on the ground watching the baby try to crawl, coaxing her to move and then laughing when she slid onto her belly.

His phone dinged with an incoming text, and Gabe sat up abruptly. "It's Matt," he said, once he unlocked his screen. "Looks like the background results are back sooner than expected."

"What's it say?" I asked, my own anxiety returning. The thought of that guy still out on the streets—knowing he'd been inside my home —was unnerving, to say the least.

Gabe tapped his phone a few times to open the report his friend had sent, then scowled.

So, not good, apparently.

"Talk to me," I said while tickling Savannah to make her laugh. "Tell me what it says."

"Elijah Harris was a beat cop for the DC police department," Gabe said, his tone edged with anger. "Got suspended for excessive force and put on administrative leave for an arrest that ended with the death of the suspect. That was two years ago. Then he joined the Virginia State Troopers, and it looks like he's racked up an impressive list of complaints against him here too. Asshole." He squeezed the phone so hard I was afraid it might crack.

To try to defuse the situation, I said, "Well, that's good. It proves what Alexis said in her journal about him being violent, right?"

"Yeah." He sighed. "But it doesn't prove that Harris killed her."

"Is there anything else in there we can use?"

"Maybe." Gabe frowned and scrolled some more. "Looks like there's a traffic-cam picture of Harris in Charles Town the night of the murder. It's close enough to Alexis's place that he could've been there at the time she was killed. But I don't know if it's enough to over-come the police department's inclination to have each other's backs."

"Damn it."

"Yeah." He sighed and turned the phone off, then sat on the couch. "But you're right. At least it's something. More than we had before, anyway. We can at least show the investigators that he was in the area that night and put him on their radar."

"So, we go to police headquarters tomorrow?"

"Yep." He tucked his phone away.

We both gazed at Savannah in silence. Everything was stacked against us. I thought about Elijah Harris, about what he was capable of, and shuddered. We were about to head into battle.

The feeling of Gabe's hand on top of mine jolted me. "Hey. Stop worrying."

So I did my best.

THIRTEEN

"**W**ow. Thank you folks for putting in all this work," Detective Anthony Marranto said.

I knew how to build a persuasive case, so of course the man was impressed. I'd laid out everything on the table in the interrogation room they'd showed us to. The pictures I'd taken of Alexis's front door, the journal we'd found, the pacifier from the floor beneath Charlotte's bedroom window, the background check stuff Matt had dug up for me on Elijah Harris. All of it.

"Unfortunately, it still doesn't amount to a slam dunk," he continued.

The restlessness inside me that had been growing since the day before exploded into full-blown impatience. "What exactly do you need to make it a 'slam dunk'?" I asked, using air quotes because yeah. I was pissed and didn't give a shit anymore about being respectful. "Because from where I'm sitting, this is starting to sound like a case of 'covering up for one of our own.'"

The detective blinked at me a moment while Charlotte stared a hole through the side of my head. Okay. Fine. Maybe I'd crossed the line there, but dammit. I was sick of spinning my wheels.

"Tony," a voice from out in the hall called. "Take a break."

I had no idea who the man filling the doorway was, but from all the stripes on his uniform, he had to be fairly high-ranking. The detective got up and walked out, giving me a final hard look over his shoulder before the door closed behind him.

"Harpers Ferry Police Chief Ed Wharton," the newcomer said, extending a hand toward me. He looked maybe sixty, with gray hair and sharp blue eyes that seemed vaguely familiar. We shook hands, and then he took the seat Tony had vacated, his expression thoughtful. "You don't remember me, do you, son?"

I frowned. "No. Sorry. Should I?"

"Back when I was a deputy, I was the one who had to tell you about your family."

Shit. Yep. I remembered those eyes now. They'd been so sad the day he'd told me about the accident. And just like that, I was back there again, on that porch, feeling like the earth had vanished beneath my feet and I was in free fall. Reality started to slip away as the past took over my mind. Thankfully, Charlotte slipped her hand into mine and squeezed, anchoring me back in the now.

Chief Wharton glanced down at the evidence we'd brought in, then back to me, his tone serious. "Look, son. You have my word we'll investigate all of this. I take the Alexis Barnes case very seriously, and I will personally make sure that there's no stone unturned here. No cover-ups of any kind." He cleared his throat and picked up the photo of Alexis and Elijah together. "Law enforcement officer or not, we've been looking for leads in that case, and this one seems as plausible as anything else we've come up with so far."

It was all too much. The flashback to the worst day of my life, the suspicion that I was up against the thin blue line despite what the chief said… the room was suddenly twenty degrees hotter than when we'd first come in. I needed to get out of there so I could breathe again. With less grace than I would've liked, I stood and shook the chief's hand, muttering my thanks before tugging Charlotte down the hall and out of the police station.

The ride home was tense. I was still trying to sort through all the emotions seeing Wharton again had brought up inside me… and, well, I wasn't the most touchy-feely guy in the world when it came to my feelings anyway.

Fine, I sucked at feelings. I'd been so overwhelmed after my family died that I found the best way to cope—the only way, really—was to ignore them until they went away. Eventually, that kind of bit me in the ass. Because now, sometimes, I found it hard to feel anything at all.

Except now, back here in Harpers Ferry, with Charlotte.

Lately I felt all sorts of shit. Some good, some bad.

And it was driving me up a wall. Like an itch beneath my skin I couldn't scratch. I wanted it to go away. I wanted to be numb again. But I feared that, now those emotions were out of the bottle, I'd never be able to stuff them back inside.

When we stopped at Charlotte's mom's house to pick up Savannah, I waited in the car because I wasn't in the mood to make nice with anyone. Charlotte didn't argue, maybe sensing how on edge I was. She was good at that. Reading me. Knowing what I needed before I knew myself. My chest squeezed a little tighter. Not because I couldn't breathe, but because of something else. Something I didn't want to examine too closely right then.

Soon, Charlotte was back with Savannah and we were on our way home. I wasn't sure when I'd started thinking of Charlotte's place as home, but it didn't mean anything. Nope. It had started raining, the weather matching my mood.

I pulled into her driveway and cut the engine, then got out to unlock the front door and check inside while Charlotte got Savannah out of her car seat. Everything was clear, but I still felt uneasy, like it was just a matter of time until something exploded. Sometimes, when we were out on missions, I'd get this way. Prowling around, looking for a fight, needing a release for all the tension inside me.

At those times, I'd go out and do some shooting practice if I could. Or I'd take a run to burn off my excess energy. Thunder rolled outside, and I sighed. Looked like a run was out.

Charlotte hurried in with the baby, and I closed and locked the door behind them.

"I'm going to get her down for her nap," she said, heading down the hall, and I stalked into the kitchen to grab a beer.

I needed to blot everything out, to forget about what I'd been through. Each time I closed my eyes, all I could see was the cemetery. The lilies and the manicured grass atop the graves and the memories of my family's faces blurring like watercolors, swimming around in my head until it was a muddy mess.

Now I could add Chief Wharton to that picture, his sad blue eyes that day. The hole in my chest where my heart had been, now hollow and empty and black as night. Would I ever be normal again? Would I ever feel human? Would I ever be able to put all this behind me and move on and—

"Savannah's already asleep," Charlotte said from beside me. I hadn't even heard her come into the kitchen. She watched me warily, like she wasn't sure if she should get any closer. Probably for the best. I was a mess, and one touch from her could make me do something I'd regret in the morning.

"Thirsty?" she asked, hiking her chin toward the now-empty beer bottle in my hand. Fuck. I didn't even remember drinking it. Not good. I set the bottle aside and stared out the window instead of answering, because what the hell could I say? She watched me a second, then said, "You can talk to me, you know? About anything. I'm here for you, Gabe."

I opened my mouth, closed it, then opened it again. Part of me wanted to take her up on her offer, tell her about what was happening inside me, see if she could help. But the rest of me was still stuck in the past, stuck in the old lies that men didn't feel shit and if they did, they never talked about it. I ended up shrugging.

Charlotte sighed and moved away, tidying the counters and table. From the corner of my eye, I watched her hips sway. That body. Those legs. What I wouldn't do to feel them wrapped around me.

And what the fuck was I doing, thinking about that right now? I was only here long enough to deal with this paternity stuff, and then I'd be gone. Charlotte was grieving the loss of her friend, and we were working together to make sure the guy who killed Alexis paid for his crime. That was all.

My body had other ideas, my cock twitching in my jeans when Charlotte bent over to load the dishwasher. Shit. The woman made chores look sexy.

Overseas, there'd been plenty of times when getting laid had been an acceptable substitute for a good run or a stint at the firing range. But sleeping with Charlotte was a complication I didn't need on top of all the others I had to deal with here.

Sex wouldn't help anything, even if my stupid brain couldn't seem to stop imagining it. The way she'd feel in my arms, the sound of her breath catching when I kissed her and stroked her, the scent of her arousal.

Unaware of the direction of my thoughts, she moved in beside me at the sink, her arm brushing mine and sending zings of awareness through me. My throat dried, and the air evaporated from my lungs. "It's really coming down out there," she said, leaning over the sink to peer out the window, and damn if that superb ass of hers wasn't right there, like it was begging me to touch it.

I swallowed hard enough for it to make a clicking noise and turned away—away from temptation, away from what would certainly be a mistake.

"Can we talk about this, please?" she said from behind me, her voice sounding as impatient as I felt.

"What?" I asked, the word cracking before I cleared my throat and tried again. My pulse was hammering now, and my ears rang from the blood rushing through my veins. I was in a bad way. Horny, hot, and hurting. My best bet was either jacking off or a cold shower, but fuck. I couldn't seem to get my feet to move.

Before I knew what I was doing, I turned back to face her, and that was a major error because she looked like my every fantasy come to life. All long lines and soft curves—and her cheeks were pink. Was she blushing? Or was she as turned on as I was?

I gripped the chair next to me to keep myself from reaching for her.

She moved closer, like she didn't care if I scorched her. She had to know she was playing with fire. Her cheeks were definitely flushed now, and her eyes glittered with heat. She was feeling this, too, no matter how ill-advised it might be. A tiny rational part of my brain yelled for me to run, to get out of there, to keep things between us strictly platonic. But the rest of my body was having none of it, because I stayed right where I was, even as she got closer and closer, until her heat and the sweet scent of her perfume surrounded me.

Her breath was warm against my temple as she cupped my cheek and whispered, "I know you're upset, Gabe. I'm upset too. Maybe we can make each other feel better."

My eyes closed, and I held my breath, struggling for the last shreds of my self-control. If this was happening, I needed to be sure we were both on the same page.

"I want to fuck you."

The words were purposely harsh. If I let myself feel everything that was rushing around inside me, I'd ruin it all. This needed to be sex, nothing more. I couldn't let it be anything more, because soon I'd be gone and she'd be here alone.

If Charlotte was shocked by my vulgarity, she didn't show it.

"Yes, please."

For a second I wasn't sure if I'd heard her correctly, but then she kissed me.

Our last kiss had been out of this world, but this one blew my universe apart. Neither of us seemed able to get enough, hands and tongues and bodies all straining for more. We stumbled down the hall, mouths locked together, and fell through my bedroom door before I bumped it closed behind us, careful not to wake the baby in the room down the hall.

Then her hands were tugging my shirt off and my fingers were fumbling on the zipper of her jeans and our breaths were ragged, as the storm outside rivaled the one brewing between us. Eventually we were both naked, writhing against each other on the bed until I pinned her beneath me and began kissing and licking and nuzzling her all over. It had been so long, too long, since I'd been with anyone this way, but there was more to my overwhelming need for her.

There was just something about Charlotte, like she was made for me.

She shuddered as I worshipped her breasts, taking first one then the other of her pretty pink nipples into my mouth, licking and sucking them until she clutched my hair and begged me for more. Only then did I continue down to the wet heat between her legs. Tore her lace thong off with my teeth, then buried my face on her slick folds. She tasted sweeter than anything I'd ever imagined. While I licked her most sensitive flesh, I inserted first one, then two fingers inside her slick, tight channel, preparing her for me as I brought her to climax again and again, then nursed her back down to earth before kissing my way back up her body to her delectable mouth.

"You are so gorgeous," I whispered against her cheek, loving how she shivered against me, sleepy and sated now. I loved everything about her, really, but I wasn't going there. My cock felt ready to explode inside my jeans, and I rubbed against her as she reached down to cup me through the fabric.

"No, you are," she said, nuzzling my neck as she stroked me. It felt too good. If she kept that up, it'd be over too fast. I pulled her hand away and kissed her palm, then pushed off the bed to remove my jeans and put on a condom.

The look in her eyes as she gave me a once-over, her gaze snagging on my hard cock, made me feel like the luckiest man on earth. Maybe we'd regret this tomorrow, but damn if I wasn't all here for it tonight. After all, another day was never guaranteed. I'd learned that the hard way.

Sorrow swelled in my chest again, but I shoved it aside. Nothing was going to get in the way of what was happening between us.

Grinning, I climbed back on the bed and straddled her, bending down to kiss her once more. "Are you ready for me?"

"Oh yeah." Charlotte smiled up at me, then pulled me down for another kiss as she wrapped those legs of hers around me just like I'd fantasized in the kitchen, digging her heels into my butt as I nudged her wet entrance with the tip of my cock before sinking hilt-deep inside her. We both held still for a moment. She was so hot and tight. For a second, I feared I'd come right then, but I waited, thought of baseball stats and battle plans and anything else boring and mundane until the urge passed.

Then I began to move, slow and steady, angling myself to hit the spot inside her that made her squirm and moan and cry out again and again. She responded like she couldn't get enough of me, and it made me wild.

There was no way I could hold back, but I needed to make her come for me again. Charlotte arched beneath me, and when I reached down to stroke her slick folds, *bam*. Her body milked mine as she came hard, and I was right behind her, slamming home once, twice, and then my balls tightened and my world exploded into a million pieces of glorious light and heat.

Next thing I knew, my head was nestled on her chest, between her beautiful breasts. Her fingers were in my hair, stroking my scalp. I wanted to say something, knew I should say something, but my brain felt muddled and I didn't want to ruin this moment of peace and tranquility after so many hours of emotional torment. Charlotte must've felt the same, because soon her breath evened out into sleep, and I followed her close behind.

FOURTEEN

The doorbell rang while I was making lunch, startling me out of my distracted thoughts. Things with Gabe were good. Maybe too good. I kept waiting for the inevitable shoe to drop. I cared for him, a lot. I hesitated to use the L word because, well, it wasn't something I'd ever thought I'd want or need in my life.

Then Gabe had shown up, and everything had changed. Since we'd made love, it was like he was a part of me now. There were reminders of him everywhere, and it was getting harder and harder to keep focused on a future without him in it. We'd still see each other because of Savannah, of course, but I needed to remember that he was leaving soon and I'd be on my own again, with the baby.

Being alone had never bothered me before. I knew I could do it. But the question was, did I want to?

The fact that I was questioning the plans I'd made for the future troubled me almost as much as the fact that Elijah was stalking us.

Ring.

Gabe and I exchanged a look, then glanced at the door. Savannah seized the opportunity to bang her hand atop the tray on her high chair, sending pureed beef flying. Food splattered everywhere, mainly all over Gabe. I bit my lip and looked at the door. "Should I get it?"

He cursed under his breath and stood to grab a towel from the counter. "Be sure to check the peephole first. If it's someone you don't know, don't open it."

My heart hammered as I peeked out. On the porch I saw the social worker who'd been handling Savannah's case. "It's Mrs. Thompson," I called to him, then opened the door. "Uh, hi. I wasn't expecting you."

"I'm sorry," she said, smiling. "I did try to call earlier, and I left several messages. Then I decided to stop by and see if you were here."

"Oh." Damn. I'd silenced my phone earlier when I'd put Savannah down for a nap so it didn't wake her, and I'd forgotten to turn the ringer back on again. "Sorry. Busy day."

"No problem. I'm just glad you're here. I normally hate doing random visits, because people tend to freak out a bit when a case worker shows up on their doorstep, but…"

Yeah. Like I was starting to freak out now. My bottom lip trembled slightly, and I bit it to keep it still, then asked, "So, what's up?"

"May I come in, Ms. Rhodes?" Mrs. Thompson said, giving me another warm smile that helped take the edge off my anxiety. "I have news on the DNA results. Is Mr. Kelley here too?"

"Please come in—we've been anxious to hear the results. And yes, he's here," I said, stepping back, then glancing over my shoulder to where Gabe was in the kitchen, feeding the baby. I gave him a pointed stare, and the second he saw the social worker, he froze, then stood and picked up Savannah to join us in the living room. Blood rushed through my ears, making it hard to hear and even harder to act normal, but I did my best. I led Mrs. Thompson into the living room. "Please have a seat."

"Thank you." Mrs. Thompson sat, putting her leather bag down by her feet. Gabe and I sat on the sofa across from her, sudden tension curdling the air. Unaware of the significance of the moment, Savannah continued gurgling happily on Gabe's lap, gnawing and drooling on the fingers of one hand while beating his leg with a stuffed toy with the other, an orange splotch of pureed apricots on one of her little cheeks. I licked my thumb and reached over to clean it off her skin, then cleared my throat and whispered to Gabe, "She has the paternity test results."

"Oh," he said, frowning down at the top of the baby's head like it took him a second to register that. Then he looked up at me, his eyes wide. "Oh!"

Luckily, Mrs. Thompson seemed like an old hand at this, and she put us out of our misery fast. "Normally the lab calls directly, but after everything that's happened, I wanted to deliver the news myself. I hope that's okay. Congratulations, Mr. Kelley. According to our test results, you are the biological father of Savannah Barnes."

For a second, we both blinked at her. Then Gabe's scowl transformed into a grin so wide, I thought his face might split in two. He stood and whooped so loud that Savannah squeaked with surprise, while I sat there trying to take it all in. Gabe was Savannah's father. That was good. Better than good. That was everything.

Next thing I knew, Gabe had pulled me up too. He had Savannah in one arm and me in the other, and he was twirling us around and laughing with pure joy. It was like something out of a corny cable movie, but man, it felt good and real and true.

On top of that, I'd thought Gabe was gorgeous before, but seeing him so open and happy, after what we'd shared the other night about closing ourselves off... Well, it was a sight to behold. His mood was contagious, and soon I was grinning like a fool too. Even Mrs. Thompson was on her feet, clapping and smiling.

Maybe there was something to be said for letting people close after all.

"So what happens next?" Gabe asked, once we'd all sat down again.

"Well, there'll be a custody hearing," Mrs. Thompson said, smoothing a hand down her skirt. "But it shouldn't be any more than a formality."

A new thought burst my happiness bubble. "What about the other petition? From Elijah Harris?" His name stuck in my throat like a cancerous lump.

"He dropped his petition this morning, after the lab called him with his results." Mrs. Thompson's smile faded. "Your custody is basically a done deal, Mr. Kelley. Blood relations are typically given custody unless there's powerful evidence to show that the child might be harmed if placed with them. Those test results will therefore factor heavily into any decision made by the courts."

"Right." Gabe reached over and took my hand, squeezing it reassuringly. "Well, that's good, then."

"It's excellent," Mrs. Thompson agreed.

"Can I get you some coffee or tea?" I offered, realizing I was being a horrible host. "We should have champagne or something to celebrate." Then I remembered, "Crap, except I don't have any here. There's some at the tavern, though, if you want to wait. I can run down and pick up a bottle."

"Oh, no. No." Mrs. Thompson checked her watch, then stood, her smile warm. "Thank you for offering, Ms. Rhodes, but I really need to get back to my office. Busy day. Besides, drinking on the clock is frowned upon, so..."

"Right. Sorry." I waited while she gathered her bag and said goodbye to Gabe and Savannah before following her to the door. "Well, thank you for coming over to let us know in person. It's wonderful news, and we really appreciate all you've done for us during this process. It's not easy."

"No. It's not. But it's very much worth it. And you're welcome, Ms. Rhodes. Congratulations again," Mrs. Thompson said before leaving.

I kept myself together until I locked the door.

"This is fantastic!" Gabe said from behind me, dancing Savannah around the living room again. "I can't believe how wonderful it feels, knowing I'm her dad. I never wanted to be a father, but I've never felt so relieved in my life. We did it, sweetheart," he said to Savannah, who was obliviously cooing and squeaking in response. "You're mine, and I'm never letting you go!" He then blew a raspberry on her tummy, which made her giggle.

I leaned back against the door, watching them, smiling. It *was* fantastic. Perfect, even. But in the recesses of my brain a spot of darkness spread, blotting out the light. Our conversation from the other night crept back in. About how he kept everyone at bay so it wouldn't hurt too much if he lost them.

And yes, he seemed happy and content now, here with the baby and me. But what happened when it was time for him to rejoin his SEAL team? He was still in the military, which meant he'd have to go when they called him back on deployment.

Sure, we'd opened up to each other while he'd been here. Shared things, more than just our bodies. Our thoughts, our feelings, our hopes, our dreams. Even so, I had the feeling that he was holding something back from me. Maybe he always would. Maybe it was his way of getting one step closer to goodbye.

But I didn't want to ruin the moment, so I kept those shadows to myself for now. I changed subjects entirely, trying to keep the light mood going. "We need to go to the grocery store this afternoon. Savannah's nearly out of formula and baby food, and the pantry's almost empty."

Savannah squealed again, waving her little arms around, all but vibrating with energy. It was clear that all the excitement had over-stimulated her, which meant strapping her into a car seat would not go well for anyone. I winced.

"Or maybe I'll go by myself, and you can stay here with her," I said, heading for the kitchen to make a list. "Anything in particular you want me to pick up? Snacks you like? A certain kind of cereal?"

When he didn't answer, I turned to find he'd followed me into the kitchen. He put Savannah back into her seat before giving me a look.

"What?" I frowned, checking the fridge and scribbling down things we needed. From his concerned expression, I knew he was thinking about Elijah Harris. I scowled. "Don't worry. It'll be fine. Nothing's happened since the break-in. And we reported everything to the police, so they're looking into him. Besides, I refuse to let that man affect my life any more than he already has."

When he still didn't respond—simply stood there with his arms crossed, watching me—I threw up my hands in exasperation. "So, what? I let him make me afraid all the time? Because that's what's happening here. I can't—" I turned away to face the sink, blinking hard against the sting in my eyes. It was frustrating as hell. I was so tired of looking over my shoulder all the time, expecting to see the boogeyman there.

Gabe came up behind me and placed his hands on my shoulders, kneading gently, his lips resting against my scalp, his breath stirring my hair. He didn't say anything, simply let me know he had my back. Okay. Yes, he was right. Once I'd calmed down a bit, forced that hunted, haunted feeling down deeper again, I could admit it. I hung my head and took a deep breath. "Fine." From behind us, Savannah squeaked again, banging her tiny fists on the tray of her carrier seat, and I smiled. "Besides, it's better not to drag the baby through a grocery store when it's clear she won't be happy about it. Let's stay home. We'll go another time."

Except we were down to the last can of formula, and it wouldn't last more than a day. And the selection of jarred baby food was growing thin as well.

"What about delivery?" Gabe asked. "I know it's not perfect, but…"

"They haven't started that here yet." I sighed. "There's been talk over the past year, but things move slow in small towns."

"I'll go," he said. "I won't have my daughter running out of things she needs."

I turned around to face him, frowning. "Wait a minute. Are you saying that because you don't want to stay here with a fussy baby?"

"Maybe," he conceded, having the decency to look sheepish. I crossed my arms and narrowed my gaze, and he grinned. "Okay. Fine. Guilty. Now finish making your list so I know what to get."

I wanted to argue on principle, but in the end I couldn't. I hated grocery shopping. That's why I waited until basically everything ran out before going. Fussy or not, Savannah beat a trip to the Piggly Wiggly any day. "Fine." I slipped the keys off the hook on the wall and tossed them to him. "You can go. But you better get everything I tell you to. And make sure you check the produce. Don't just grab the first ones you see."

Half an hour later, I was sitting at the table with Savannah, and Gabe was tugging on his jacket. He bent and gave me a kiss, then kissed the top of his daughter's head before heading out the door. "Keep the house locked up while I'm gone."

"Yes, sir," I said, giving him a faux-military salute, then called behind him, almost as an afterthought, "You be careful too."

FIFTEEN

Careful was my middle name. Or at least it felt like it most days.

I backed out of Charlotte's driveway and headed into town. The day was overcast, the brisk fall air a hint of what was to come. The two-lane highway into Harpers Ferry had been repaved recently, by the looks of it, making the yellow and red leaves stand out even more against the black asphalt.

The radio in the SUV was tuned to a country station, and while the singer crooned on about the man who'd done her wrong, I let my mind drift to the news I'd just learned.

I was a dad. Savannah was my daughter.

Holy shit.

I still couldn't stop grinning about it, even if it did complicate things even more. I needed to call my CO when I got back from the store and tell him. Smith would be happy for me, I thought. He had kids of his own, so…

For a moment, a weird ache filled my chest. In other circumstances, in other lifetimes, now would be the time people would call their parents, their families, to share the happy news. But my family was gone.

I'd figured I'd put that to rest, finally come to terms with the loss, when I'd gone to the graveyard, yet it kept cropping up at the weirdest, most inopportune times. Like when I heard a certain song. Or when I passed a sign along the road for a place I'd once gone to with my mom and dad and Isaac. Or now. When one of the most momentous occasions of life had happened, and the most important people weren't there to share it with me.

That feeling had only happened a few times before. My high school graduation. The day I'd passed SEAL training.

Which brought me back to my present dilemma. Now that I knew for certain Savannah was mine, there were decisions to be made. Things I needed to figure out. I'd been with my SEAL team for ten years now, and it was pretty much my life.

I'd eaten, drunk, and breathed that life for so long, I really didn't know anything else. Everything was regimented. Everything had a timeline, a purpose, rules and regulations associated with it. I liked that. Liked knowing exactly what I'd be doing that day when I woke —even if what I'd be doing was a completely unpredictable extraction or other mission. Even then, it still had the framework I'd been trained in, and I had the rest of my team around me. Not having to worry about making major decisions, because that all came down to me through the chain of command. They told me where to go, what to do, who to be.

Now, though, that was gone, at least while I was home. And it felt weird. Disconcerting.

And more than a little scary, truth be told.

Being a civilian meant making all those choices yourself. Meant forging ahead, not knowing what the future held or how you'd get there. All those rules and regulations, gone. Charlotte seemed to do fine with it. Most people did. But I'd spent my whole adult life with the other scenario, so how was I going to proceed going forward? Could I adjust to civilian life?

I rounded a curve in the road and glanced in the rearview mirror. Uh-oh. My stomach sank as my instincts went on high alert. It being early afternoon on a Wednesday, there wasn't much traffic, so the fact that the same truck had been following me since I left Charlotte's house did not go unnoticed. Black. Nondescript, with tinted windows that prevented me from easily seeing the driver. Because of course.

Fuck.

Frowning, I straightened in my seat and increased my speed, just to see what would happen. Sure enough, the truck behind me sped up, too, not right on my ass, but close enough to see where I was going and act accordingly. Shit. I'd picked up a tail.

As I wound through the road's curves and hairpin turns, the vehicle behind me gradually crept closer and closer until it was right on my ass. Other vehicles passed in the opposite direction, semis and cars and even a few motorcycles, and pretty soon, the asshole was crowding me on the tight roadway.

To my left was the other lane of traffic, then a guardrail to keep motorists from plunging off the sheer drop to nowhere. To my right was mountain. Which basically meant I had nowhere to go.

Fuck. Time for evasive maneuvers.

We went around another tight curve. By then, I was going faster than I should've been, but dammit, I needed to get out of there, and the only way was through. And that's when the asshole behind me made his move. I was fairly certain it was a "he," because, c'mon. It had to be

Harris, right? He honked his horn, then nudged my back bumper with his front one.

I tightened my grip on the steering wheel to stay on the road, and thank God nothing was coming the other direction. I managed to keep in my lane and pressed the accelerator to put some distance between us again, heart slamming against my rib cage and lungs tight. Unfortunately, it didn't help much, since Harris sped up too and rammed me again, this time harder, sending me screeching across the other lane—still amazingly empty—and careening toward the guardrail.

Time seemed to slow, and it all felt like it was happening to someone else. I'd had this happen before, usually on the battlefield, when adrenaline seared through my veins and my vision tunneled to just the here, just the now, just survival. Through sheer force of will I managed to avoid smashing through the guardrail and plummeting to my death. I sucked in a huge gulp of oxygen and dug my heels into the floorboards, my mind racing along with the car's engine.

Oh God. Oh God. Oh God.

Memories flashed before my eyes, blending with the scene unfolding before me. This was exactly how my family had died. My dad had lost control during a rainstorm and gone off the road, killing them all. I couldn't die like that. I'd had nightmares for years that I'd been in the car with them that day, tumbling and tumbling and tumbling as the world shattered and their screams sliced into my brain like a scalpel.

Chest constricted and eyes scratchy, I squinted out the windshield and spotted a hiking trail parking lot up ahead. Thank fuck. Thank fuck it was also empty, meaning I could swerve into it fast. I did, then slammed on the brakes, praying it would be enough to get this asshole off my tail.

It was. Harris didn't have time to react, and there wasn't enough room for him to turn around. With a squeal of rubber, he sped onward toward town. I sat there for a while, getting my shit together again and letting the adrenaline burn out of my system so my hands weren't shaking so badly.

Several minutes and more than a few deep breaths later, I was relatively under control again. I pulled out and continued into town, keeping an eye out for the other vehicle. I figured Harris was smart enough not to try that shit again, but maybe he was cocky. Maybe he thought being law enforcement put him above the law himself. Maybe he'd mess up.

Sure enough, once I'd crossed into the town limits, I spotted his truck parked along a side street. I slowed enough to snap a picture of his license plate with my phone. I didn't want to confront him, not yet, seeing as I was unarmed. But this wasn't over. Not by a long shot. I circled the block, clearing my head and calming my raging pulse, before looping back to the grocery store, keeping an eye out behind me to make sure he wasn't about to try anything else.

If Harris was stupid enough to come back for a second try, though, at least I'd be mentally prepared for battle.

I walked through the store in a daze, trying to focus on the list when all I wanted to do was go into war mode. I didn't want Charlotte to see that side of me, at least not yet, and by the time I pulled into the driveway again, I thought I had myself pretty well under control. But then I walked inside and Charlotte stopped in the middle of the living room, her eyes wide.

"What's wrong?" she asked, walking over to where I stood at the door, my arms laden down with bags. "You look like you've seen a ghost."

I took the bags to the kitchen, trying to figure out what to tell her, but the words wouldn't come. So, instead, I gestured for her to follow me outside. We walked down to the SUV to grab the last of the groceries, and I pointed at the damaged back bumper.

"What the fuck?" she asked, staring down at the caved-in tailgate. "Did someone hit you in the parking lot?" Charlotte straightened, her cheeks flushed and her eyes sparkling with anger. "This is exactly why I hate going to that place! People don't look where they're going and drive like jackasses. I'm going to call them and have them check their security cam—"

"No," I managed. I needed to keep it together. "It didn't happen at the store. Someone tried to run me off the road on my way there."

"What?" Charlotte froze then, all the color draining from her face. "Oh God. Elijah."

"Yep. Don't know anyone else who'd do it," I said, looping the last bag over my arm, then closing the back hatch with a loud *thump*.

I was used to war zones, sniper fire, night raids where the odds were stacked against us and one wrong move could take out an entire unit. What I wasn't used to was coming close to dying the same way I'd lost my entire family. I never wanted Savannah to feel that sort of pain. Fucking Elijah Harris. My earlier fear had given way to fury. "I got a picture of his license plate. But he's not stupid, and I'd bet good money if we ran it, it wouldn't come back to him."

Charlotte shook her head, then hugged me, squeezing me tight for a second before letting me go. I savored that warmth, fleeting though it was. "Shit. Shit!" she said. She looked around before following me inside, like she was checking for an interloper. "We need to call the police anyway. Let them know what happened, even if they say it was just a hit-and-run. They can add it to his file."

"Yep." I took off my jacket, then kissed Savannah's head before dialing the chief's number. I filled him in on what happened, then sent him the photo of the license plate, along with a couple more of the damage to the bumper that I took in the driveway while on the call with him.

We were silent as we put the groceries away. I could tell Charlotte was scared and was probably thinking about all the ways Elijah Harris could harm us.

Me? I was mapping out my battle strategy. No way was he going to get close to us again.

SIXTEEN

We sat down to our dinner of spaghetti with Bolognese sauce and garlic bread, the air heavy with what was to come. Gabe was quieter than usual.

He was doing his best to act like nothing was wrong, but I could tell that he was still working through the incident on the road. The parallels to what had happened to his family weren't lost on me. I couldn't blame him for needing some time to process it. Plus, the custody hearing was tomorrow morning. It should be a simple formality, but on top of everything else that was going on...

Savannah seemed to have found her outside voice and let out a screech that cut through some of the tension. Gabe chuckled and reached over to fluff the dark curls on her head before twirling some spaghetti on his fork. "So, about tomorrow." He chewed and swallowed, then frowned into his bottle of beer. "I have something to ask you."

My nerves flared. I wasn't sure why, but I had the feeling that whatever he was going to say would change my life forever. There'd been a lot of that lately, it seemed. "Sure," I said, wiping my mouth with a napkin. "What do you need?"

He didn't answer right away, taking more interest than was necessary in his food. Finally, he took a deep breath and met my gaze, his own intense enough to make my pulse kick higher. "I want to ask if you'll be Savannah's legal guardian. Just until she's old enough to be in school. Then I can have her with me on base." I must've given him a strange look, because he added, "They're very safe places for kids, but I'm not exactly in a position career-wise to take her with me now. I mean, the places I'm sent on missions aren't exactly spots where you can have family with you. In a few years, maybe I can get a promotion, a desk job at the Pentagon or something, but right now, it's not feasible."

I blinked at him as my mind worked through it all.

"I know you love her," he said, when I didn't respond right away. "And I can't imagine anyone I'd trust more to keep her safe."

Honored. Shocked. Terrified. Thrilled. Emotions flooded through me as I tried to figure out how to answer him. I absolutely loved Savannah like she was my own child. I'd do anything for her. But being her guardian felt an awful lot like being her mom, and…

No. Don't go there.

Gabe was asking me to raise Savannah *for* him, not *with* him.

As much as it pained me to recognize that fact, I couldn't say no to him.

He watched me from across the table. Still intense, still gorgeous, still Gabe in all his earnest, heartfelt glory. And damn. How could I turn him down?

I couldn't.

"Okay. Yes." I exhaled slowly. "I'd be honored to be Savannah's guardian."

His smile, slow and sweet, made my breath catch. "Thank you."

Then he was leaning across the table and kissing me, and that was all that mattered.

I arrived at the Jefferson County Courthouse at 8:45 a.m. sharp the next morning, with Charlotte by my side. Having her agree to be Savannah's guardian had been a huge relief and supplied the final piece of the plan I'd been constructing for weeks to present to the judge.

My pulse was racing, and I was already sweating from nerves, despite the cool day outside. The social worker, Mrs. Thompson, had assured us that this should be nothing more than a formality, since Alexis was dead and the DNA results proved I was Savannah's father, but I was still afraid I'd screw it up somehow.

"Relax," Charlotte said, nudging me with her shoulder. "You look like a dead man walking."

Faking a smile, I let go of her hand to carry Savannah through the metal detector at the entrance to the courthouse lobby, then waited while Charlotte was screened. On top of the stress of the hearing, being in that courthouse was bringing back memories I'd thought I'd locked away a long time ago. Memories of being a grieving teenager dealing with the court system in the aftermath of the accident. There'd been wills and probate and judges deciding the best place for me to live until I turned eighteen. Some of it was a blur. Some of it lived on in the sick twisting my gut was doing right now.

At least Savannah was young enough that she wouldn't remember any of this stuff. I kissed her hair and adjusted her in my right arm, the file of paperwork I'd completed tucked under the left.

"Come on." I waited as Charlotte grabbed the diaper bag off the X-ray conveyor belt and slung it over her shoulder. I was so grateful to have her with me today, and not merely because she was an extra set of hands to help care for Savannah during all this. I'd only been home a short time, a few weeks, and yet somehow in that time, Charlotte had become my rock: the person I looked forward to seeing first thing in the morning and the last person I wanted to see at night. We talked, laughed, and comforted each other... and the sex was amazing. I didn't want to read too much into any of that, but I couldn't imagine going through any of this without her.

We walked through the lobby, past office doors lining either side of the space, our footsteps echoing off the marble floor. The murmur of voices filled the air, and in the distance, through a set of open double doors, I saw the grand courtroom, a huge, airy space with a large circular chandelier hanging over the center and the judge's bench at the end of it all.

Thankfully, my hearing wasn't going to be in there. We were going to the judge's chambers, since I was the only one presenting a case, with Elijah Harris having dropped his petition.

The thought of that asshole had my blood pressure rising. I had no proof that he'd been the one trying to run me off the road yesterday. The cops hadn't found anything yet, but it would be a hell of a coincidence if Harris wasn't involved somehow. And I didn't believe in coincidences.

Out of habit, I scanned the faces of the people around us as we headed for the elevators to the second floor. I was always aware of my surroundings right off: the exits, the entrances, any potential threats. And Elijah Harris was definitely a threat.

Even though I had no evidence he'd been following us, with his law enforcement background, it was a good possibility. If I'd been in his position, that's what I'd do. And while the courthouse had good security, I wasn't taking any chances with Savannah's or Charlotte's life.

Luckily, I didn't see any sign of Harris. I jammed the elevator button, then bounced my daughter in my arms while we waited. A few minutes later, we stood outside a door marked with the name *Judge Franklin Mayhew*, and my chest squeezed tight.

"This is it," I said, a trickle of perspiration running down the back of my neck.

"Hey." Charlotte gave me a reassuring smile as she rubbed my back. "You'll be fine. Just breathe. You got this."

"Thanks."

Savannah gurgled and gnawed on the ear of the stuffed toy in her hand, oblivious to everything else.

After a deep, calming breath, I opened the door for Charlotte, then followed her inside to stand before a reception desk. An older woman finished typing something on her computer, then looked up at us over the rims of her glasses.

"May I help you?" she asked, her expression pure schoolmarm.

"Yes," I said, then cleared my throat. "My name's Gabe Kelley, and I have a custody hearing with Judge Mayhew at nine."

The woman gave a curt nod, then gestured toward some empty chairs along the wall. "Please have a seat. I'll let him know you've arrived."

In here, it was hard to tell you weren't in some normal office, with the beige walls and beige carpet and beige furniture. Beige forever. While the assistant phoned the judge and spoke in muted tones, I took a seat next to a ficus and did my best to keep Savannah from tearing all its leaves off.

God. I hated these places. It was one of the reasons I'd joined the military, to avoid getting stuck behind a desk somewhere like this.

What felt like a small eternity passed, with me still trying to get my thundering heart under control, before the woman behind the desk led us into the judge's office. I know I shouldn't have been so nervous. I'd faced down military brass and unsavory characters a lot more threatening than the gray-haired man across the desk from me. But this was about my daughter, about her future. This was about the rest of my life. Our lives. Hopefully together.

"Mr. Kelley," the judge said, standing to shake my hand. Charlotte took the folder from me so I could free up a hand. "Judge Mayhew. Nice to meet you. I remember your parents. Shame what happened."

"Thanks," I said, adjusting Savannah in my arms and ignoring the clench in my heart at the reminder of my past. I should be used to it by now, after being back here for several weeks, but it still got me every time.

"And Charlotte. Always great to see you," the judge said, smiling at her.

It seemed everyone in Harpers Ferry knew who she was too. Then again, with the tavern, I guessed that made sense. And well, Charlotte had never left town like I did, so…

I passed the folder of paperwork across the desk to the judge, hoping the slight tremor in my hands didn't show. Jesus. Me, always rock solid during any tense situation, losing my shit over a simple court hearing. Except this didn't seem simple. Not at all. It felt like the biggest moment in my life.

Because yeah, I'd helped conceive Savannah, but the outcome of this hearing would determine whether I'd finally become her legal father.

"And this must be Savannah," the judge said, grinning at my daughter, then reaching out to take her hand. "I've got grandkids about your age, sweetheart. What a good girl."

"She is," Charlotte and I said together, then gave each other some side-eye.

"Right," Judge Mayhew said. We all took our seats, and then he opened the folder and frowned down at my paperwork. "Let's get this started."

While he read through everything, I looked around, trying to distract myself. The office was small, maybe ten by fifteen, with two of the walls lined with bookcases. Leatherbound books with gold lettering on the spines crowded together, mainly law-related from what I could tell. There were a few pictures of the judge and a woman I presumed was his wife. A few more with what were probably adult children and those grandkids he'd mentioned.

Charlotte reached over and put her hand on my knee to stop me from bouncing my heel on the floor. Damn. I did that when I was nervous. I hadn't realized I was doing it now. For her part, she looked serene and cool. I felt hot and buzzing, like I'd swallowed a hive of bees.

"I see here that you're an active duty Navy SEAL, is that correct?" The judge looked up at me over his wire-rimmed glasses.

"Yes, sir." I swallowed hard.

"Well, first off, thank you for your service."

I gave a curt nod.

"And second, while as I understand it you weren't in the picture until recently, I'm sorry for your loss of the child's mother. Nasty business, that, and I hope the police wrap up the investigation soon to give you all some closure."

"Thanks." The word croaked out of my constricted throat.

He glanced down at the paperwork again, then gave me a concerned look. "I suppose the biggest question I need answered, Mr. Kelley, is how you plan to provide for your daughter while you're away on missions. From what I see of your financial records here, it seems money won't be an issue, but what about your daughter's emotional and physical needs?"

I looked at Charlotte again, and she nodded. "As you'll see in the paperwork, sir, Charlotte has agreed to be Savannah's legal guardian in my absence. The baby's mother chose Charlotte to be her godmother, so she's an important part of my daughter's life. She'll take care of Savannah while I'm away on missions. The baby has already spent time in her home and is used to her, so I don't think it will be a problem."

"Hmm." Judge Mayhew flipped through more pages before focusing on me and asking somberly, "And what happens if you don't come back?"

I blinked at him for a second, then felt Charlotte squeeze my knee. "Well, sir, then I'd want Charlotte to get custody of the baby. She's got a stable income, a stable home, and—"

"And I love Savannah like she's my own," Charlotte said, her tone impassioned. "Alexis was my best friend, sir, and there's nothing I wouldn't do to make sure Savannah has the absolute best life possible. I'd do anything to make her happy. I've also qualified to be a foster mother, so there should be no concern about Savannah's safety."

Judge Mayhew looked between the two of us, then stared at Savannah a moment before nodding. "Yes, I can see that this little girl is much loved." He sighed and closed the folder. "Based on what I've seen in the paperwork, it all looks in order. My primary concern in these cases is the best interests of the child, and you seem like a fine young man, Mr. Kelley. And I've known Charlotte all her life and know she'll make a great mother. So," he sat back and clasped his hands atop the folder. "Given that the DNA results conclusively prove your paternity of Savannah, I hereby grant you sole legal custody of your daughter, Mr. Kelley, along with guardianship rights to Charlotte. Congratulations to you both."

And just like that, I became a dad. For real.

Charlotte was standing and shaking the judge's hand, and then someone clapped me on the shoulder. But all I could do was kiss my daughter's head and breathe in her sweet baby smell, closing my eyes and thanking God and everyone else that this was over and we could move on with our lives.

SEVENTEEN

We'd been home for a few hours, relaxing after the stressful hearing, when my doorbell rang. I left Savannah and Gabe playing on the floor in the living room and went to answer the door. It was my mom, holding a bakery box in her hands.

"Congratulations!" she said, hugging me awkwardly around the large box. "I just wanted to stop by and see the new parents." She held out the box with a wink. "And I worked for hours making this for you guys."

"Thanks," I said, returning her smile. Even if the box hadn't had a sticker from Delicious Delights on it, I'd know damned well the cake came from the bakery in Charles Town. My mom never baked anything in her life. After opening the box to show off the cake inside —fluffy white icing with "Happy Custody Day" written on top in pink frosting—I took it into the kitchen and served up slices for each of us. Back in the living room, I took a seat on the sofa, while Gabe stayed on the floor with Savannah and my mom sat in one of the armchairs.

Gabe downed half his slice of cake in two bites, grinning at my mom. "This is fantastic, Mrs. Rhodes."

"Thanks." My mom beamed at him.

We chatted as we ate our cake, and then I carried the plates to the kitchen. "Gabe, are you okay with the baby? I need to go get ready for work."

"Oh, uh." He gave me a wounded-puppy look before quickly covering it behind his usual stoic facade. "Yeah. Sure. I'm good."

"I can watch the baby, if you want," my mom offered. "And Charlotte, why don't you call in sick tonight? You two deserve to celebrate on your own."

To say I was surprised was an understatement. My mom loved Savannah but was usually sick of watching her after doing it every weekday. My thoughts must've shown on my face, because next thing I knew, my mom had gotten up and joined me in the kitchen.

"Seriously, honey. I don't mind. Savannah might be the closest thing to a granddaughter that I'll get."

Ouch. I did not want to go there, so I turned away, staring down at the plates as I rinsed them off before shoving them in the dishwasher. "It's fine, Mom," I said, probably more harshly than I should have, but dammit, I was hurt and a little pissed that she'd come at me like that. "I really need to go in tonight to check on things and take care of some paperwork. Gabe's got it handled here."

"I didn't mean to upset you, honey," Mom said, lowering her voice to a whisper. "It's just that..." She sighed. "I want more for you. You know that. More than running a tavern in a small town. You have a college degree. You're smart. You could do so much more than this." She waved a hand toward the living room. "And now with Gabe here, and the baby, I thought you might..."

"Might what?" I gave her a look. "It's not like that, okay?" I didn't want it to be like that. Did I? No. That was ridiculous. Sure, Gabe and I were sleeping together. The sex was hot. Amazing. And we both loved Savannah so much. But that didn't mean we could build a life together. Didn't mean we should even try. "I need to get ready."

I went back to my room, trying to look as normal and casual as possible despite feeling like a robot. To distract myself from the ache in my heart, I closed the door and concentrated on getting ready. Mom knew I was interested in having a career, not having kids. It had never been an issue between us before.

And especially after what I'd seen her go through when I was young —she'd raised me essentially alone, my own dad popping in and out of our lives whenever he felt like it until he disappeared for good—I couldn't believe she'd put me on the spot like that. She had to see how much I'd accomplished on my own. How I didn't need anyone to make me feel like a success. I owned my own business, was in charge of my own life. What more could a woman want?

With a sigh, I stripped and put on my robe, then headed into the bathroom, turning on the old shower to let the water heat up while I scrubbed my face in the sink. Fine, maybe I did feel lonely sometimes… maybe more so since Gabe had been here to show me what it could be like with a partner around. That didn't mean I was going to give everything up to be with him. Not with him going back out with his SEAL team soon and me left behind to pick up the pieces.

Nope. Not doing that.

Been there, watched my mom go through that with me.

The one time I'd tried to have a relationship, back in high school, it had fallen apart, just like I knew it would. I'd fallen completely in love with Dustin. We'd planned to spend the rest of our lives together. Then he got accepted into a college in England, and boom, he was gone. He'd asked me to wait for him, but no. Hell no. I wasn't about to put my life on hold for anyone. Not my dad. Not Dustin. Not even Gabe now.

Steam filled the bathroom, and I turned to check the shower temperature before getting in. That's when I felt the hand on my shoulder, and I screamed. Or I would have if not for the hand over my mouth. Eyes wide with fear and heartbeat thumping in my temples, I spun to find Gabe behind me, grinning like an idiot. My terror turned to outrage in one second flat.

"What the hell?" Charlotte whispered, eyes sparkling with rage. "You scared the living shit out of me."

I chuckled, pulling her closer. Man, she felt good. All soft and curvy, even when she was pissed. "I thought maybe I could help you get ready. After we celebrate." I reached between us to undo the belt on her robe. The terry cloth parted and bared her to me. My cock hardened instantly, letting her know how much I wanted her. She looked so cute glaring up at me that I couldn't resist bending down to kiss her.

She dodged my lips, though, hissing, "My mom is out there!"

"So?" I nibbled her tense jaw before kissing my way over to her earlobe, where I nibbled some more, loving the way she shivered and shuddered against me. Charlotte couldn't resist me, and I loved it. "Are you sure you have to go to work tonight?"

Her response this time was a bit less stern and far breathier. "Yes, I'm sure." Her nails dug into my shoulders as she melted into me, the heat between her legs grinding against my straining cock and making me moan. "I've already asked my staff to cover me more than I should the past couple of weeks, and I can't expect them to do it forever."

"Hmm." I bent to kiss the tops of her breasts, then toyed with a pretty pink nipple until she squirmed and mewled into my mouth. "Well, as the boss, there's no reason you can't invite a guest to come along, right?"

Charlotte pulled back, giving me an inquiring look. "You want to come to work with me?"

I shrugged. "If you're game."

Her smile took my breath away. "Actually, I'd really like that."

"Good." I let her go to tug off my shirt, winking. "Me too. But let's go ahead and shower first, eh?"

We got naked and climbed into the shower. It was a bit small for two people, but we made it work. I couldn't get enough of her—the way she smelled, the way she tasted, the sounds she made as she came apart in my arms as I went down on her, her back to the tile wall. After her shudders had ebbed, I stood and she stroked me as the water ran over us, our mouths sealed together in a kiss to swallow my cries of passion. It felt like coming home.

By the time we got out and got dressed, her mom had settled into the sofa in the living room with Savannah on her lap. She'd put on a movie, and they were watching it together. Some cartoon with talking cars.

"Are you sure you don't mind staying tonight?" Charlotte asked once more as she pulled on her jacket. A bit of the tension around her lips had returned, I noticed, and I couldn't help wondering what this thing was between her and her mom. I knew a bit about Charlotte's past, but there seemed to be more that she wasn't telling me. I felt closer to her than to anyone else on the planet, but there still seemed to be a wall between us that I wasn't sure how to breach.

"I said it's fine, honey," her mom answered with an edge of tension in her voice.

Yep. Definitely something going on there. I'd need to ask Charlotte about it later. For now, we needed to get to the tavern.

I kissed Savannah goodbye, waved to Charlotte's mom and thanked her again, then followed Charlotte out the door.

EIGHTEEN

Rhodes Tavern was jamming.

It was Friday night, and the place was loud and busy—just how I liked it. Of course, having Gabe there didn't hurt either. He was currently sitting at the end of the bar, sipping his drink and giving me the kind of stare that made me shiver. I had to fight myself to keep from dragging him into the storeroom.

I'd been busy, filling in where needed. Directing traffic at the door. Busing tables. Mopping up messes. Generally doing whatever would help most at any given time. Now I was bartending while one of the guys took their break. It was fun, hearing all the chatter and talking with patrons. I'd always liked bartending. Something about mixing drinks was interesting to me—sort of like cooking, without the food.

Music thumped through the overhead speakers from the jukebox in the corner. It played everything from rock to pop to syrupy country ballads. Right now a bunch of people were on the dance floor in the corner doing the electric slide. I couldn't help tapping my toes as I worked behind the bar.

Gabe and I had even managed to sneak in a dance or two over the course of the night. It was nice getting out of the house for once and letting loose, even if I was working most of the time.

Speaking of letting loose, our first dance had been a fast, Macarena-style thing where I had no idea what I was doing, but that he seemed to handle pretty well. The dance floor had been packed, so at least I didn't stand out too badly, but I hadn't missed the fact Gabe had caught the attention of quite a few ladies. The man had moves. Heat crept up my cheeks as I thought about what he could do between the sheets.

But back off, ladies. He's mine.

I shook my head and grabbed another glass to start a new drink order.

Our second dance tonight was a slow song. A croon-ey ballad about love and how it changed a person, sometimes without them even knowing. While I wasn't ready to go quite that far and put the L word to what I felt toward Gabe, I had to admit what was between us was pretty great.

I glanced down the bar and met his gaze again, and my internal temperature went up a few notches. Yeah. Great indeed. We'd swayed to the music, our bodies brushing, our breath mingled, our hearts beating in time, and for a moment, I got lost in the magic. Of course, then one of the servers had interrupted us and we'd had to cut our dance short. It was a nice memory, though.

Now it was nearing last call, and I wanted to wring those last few dollars out of my customers before sending them on their way. I set two fuzzy nipples on a tray for a server, then turned to the next ticket. Four shots of tequila and a couple longnecks. Easy-peasy.

As I worked, I enjoyed the tingle of Gabe's stare on me. It made me feel wanted and wild. Made me feel protected, too, like as long as he was watching me, nothing else could touch me. Memories of us earlier, in the shower, kept flashing into my head, making me even warmer all over.

Maybe after we closed, I'd pull him down the hall to my office and we could have a repeat performance. The desk was old and wooden, but if we broke it, I'd just have to get a new one. Ha!

"Hey, boss," one of the servers called from the other end of the bar. "Can I get a couple more specials, please?"

"Sure thing." I finished with the shots and bottles, then moved on to his order. Time flew by after that, and before I knew it, the last hour was gone and we were closed. Rather than making the staff stay, I told them to go home and I'd handle the cleanup and resetting myself. I figured it was the least I could do after all they'd done for me the last few weeks.

A few servers gave me knowing looks as they walked out, their eyes flicking from me to Gabe and back again like they knew exactly what I was thinking, but I didn't care. I wanted more time alone with him.

Once they were gone, he and I went around clearing tables and filling up bins with dishes to take to the kitchen to wash and sterilize. It was nice having his help. We stood side by side at the sink, rinsing and loading glasses into the huge dishwasher I'd bought for the bar a few years back. It was kind of complicated, but once you understood it, not hard.

"I can tell you how to work it," I offered, glancing over at Gabe.

"I'd like that," he said, bending down to kiss me. "But first..." He untied the apron he'd put on, then pulled it over his head before holding out his arms to me.

I gave him a confused look. "What are you doing?"

He waggled his brows. "We need to finish our dance."

Chuckling, I shut off the water and grabbed a towel to dry my hands, my own apron splotched with water and soapsuds. "Uh, sorry, but there's no music."

That's when the singing started. Gabe was a lot of things, but a good singer wasn't one of them.

I clamped a hand over his mouth. "Please stop that. You'll scare the mice."

His laugh rang through the kitchen. "Fine. How about if I hum, then?"

"Humming is good." Honestly, I didn't need any music. Didn't need an excuse to get back in his arms either. I pulled off my own apron and stepped into his embrace, shivering as he pulled me close and nuzzled the spot beneath my ear that drove me wild with need. He hummed softly, something low and sweet, and the world reduced to only the two of us, only that moment. All my fears and doubts melted away, and I allowed myself to simply be.

I rested my head on his chest, my hand clasped in his, over his heart, and I closed my eyes, picturing what life could be like if things were different. Maybe we'd buy a bigger house here in Harpers Ferry. Gabe could start his own security business like his friend had, or he could help me run the bar. Maybe we'd have a kid of our own, a brother or sister for little Savannah. We might not have much, but we had every-thing we needed.

"Penny for your thoughts," he whispered against my temple, his breath warm and minty with a hint of the rum he'd had earlier. "You look happy."

"I am happy," I said, smiling. I had Gabe. I had Savannah. I had the tavern. Usually moments like this were a red flag that everything was about to come crashing down, but here, tonight, I felt nothing but gratitude and grace.

Standing on tiptoe, I rose until our mouths were even, and I met his gaze. "I believe, sir, that you owe me another kiss."

His slow smile turned me into a puddle of gooey desire. "Well, then. Best pay up, huh?"

Our lips had just met when the fire alarm blared.

"What the—" I pulled back from Charlotte, scowling and trying to figure out what the hell was happening. It took a second for the lust haze in my brain to wear off and for reality to snap back into place. "Shit. It's the fire alarm." I took Charlotte by the arm and pushed her toward the door to the front of house. "Get outside and call 9-1-1 —now."

"But I think it's a false alarm!" she yelled above the noise.

"Either way, we need to let the fire department know. Go!"

She turned toward the door, but the minute it swung open to the main bar area, it was clear this wasn't a false alarm. A blast of heat rushed in, and a flickering orange-red glow danced up the walls. I couldn't see any actual flames yet from where I was standing, but they were there. I was sure of it. Especially since the sinister black smoke creeping along the ceiling like a phantom was a dead giveaway.

How the fuck?

Shit. Think, dude. Think.

I squinted through the increasingly acrid air, searching for a fire extinguisher. They were required by code in all public buildings. There it was, on the wall closest to the bar. I tugged my shirt up to cover my mouth and nose and ran over to grab it, but it was too hot to touch, and the smoke was too bad now anyway.

When we'd finished cleaning up out there, maybe an hour ago, everything had been fine. Charlotte had double-checked the front doors, and they'd been locked. But sometime between when we'd come back here to do the dishes and now, a raging inferno had started. I shifted into response mode.

The smoke was building quickly. Charlotte was coughing and looked pale and shaken. I couldn't blame her. Watching the life you'd built evaporate in front of your eyes did that to a person. I should know. But we couldn't worry about the tavern now.

We had to focus on getting out of the place alive. I shook her gently to jar her out of her daze, then shouted, gesturing in case she couldn't hear me, "We can't get out the front. Let's use the back exit into the alley and call the fire department from there."

She nodded, and we struggled back through the kitchen, coughing and wheezing. Reaching the back door, I shoved hard with my shoulder.

Nothing.

I tried again, but it didn't budge. I glanced over at Charlotte, who gave me a wild-eyed look. I knew that look. I felt the same fear, but I couldn't let it take over. I had to stay calm for us to have any hope of getting out of here.

"I think it's blocked," I yelled over the rush of the flames growing ever closer and the still-blaring fire alarms. "I can't get the door open."

She just nodded, an eerily vacant look on her face, like she'd already given up.

No. Fuck no. No giving up. Not now. Not ever.

"Fuck!" Furious, I hauled off and kicked the damned door at hard as I could, but it still didn't move.

Wisps of black smoke curled down from the ceiling and inched closer to our faces like tentacles. The temperature had to be well over a hundred in there now, and my skin felt sticky and hot and too tight for my body. If we didn't get out soon, we were both going to die.

NINETEEN

From the terror in Charlotte's eyes, I knew she was seconds away from full-blown panic. She was already breathing faster and deeper than she should've been under the current conditions, and the last thing I wanted was for her to succumb to smoke inhalation.

Spotting a stack of clean towels on the counter near the sink, I ran over and soaked a couple with cool water before handing her one. "Here. Tie this around your face like a mask. It'll help you breathe easier and will filter out some of the smoke."

She blinked at me a moment, then took the towel. I couldn't tell what she was thinking, but considering we were trapped in a kitchen while her life's work burned to the ground, I could only imagine what she must be going through.

I got my towel secured, then moved behind Charlotte and brushed aside her shaking fingers to knot hers behind her head as well. Then I took her shoulders and turned her to face me, holding her gaze. Her breathing had gotten even more erratic, and I was afraid she was hyperventilating. "We're going to be all right," I said, slowly and calmly. "I promise you I'll get you out of here, okay?"

Tears gathered in her eyes, and I wanted nothing more than to gather her close and hold her until all her fears went away—but that had to come later. First, I needed to figure out how the fuck I was going to keep my promise.

A loud groan issued from the front of the bar, followed by a huge crash. The whole building shuddered. My pulse kicked into overdrive. The roar of the flames drowned out everything now, even the alarms, and while the sprinkler system had kicked in, the fire was too big to douse at that point. All I could do was pray the fire department would get here soon. I had to keep us alive until then.

Think, dude. Think.

Right. I looked over Charlotte's shoulder to the window behind the sink. It was small and faced the brick wall on the other side of the alley, but it was better than nothing. It was also reinforced security glass with wires embedded in it, which meant I'd need more than my fist to smash through it. I squeezed Charlotte's shoulders a little bit tighter and shouted, "Is there a hammer around here?"

Charlotte began digging around, rifling through all the utensil drawers, searching for something, anything I could use to smash through that glass. My skin felt puckered now from the heat, and there had to be a good foot of smoke hovering near the ceiling. If we didn't get out of there soon, we'd be cooked alive. At least we were in the kitchen.

I swallowed a bubble of inappropriate laughter down my scratchy throat. Humor was my go-to release when shit got too real. It was kind of an occupational hazard on a SEAL team.

Halfway through another drawer, she found a steel meat-tenderizing mallet and held it up. "Will this work?"

"Yes!" That would work just fine. I took the mallet from her, then climbed up on the counter, putting all my strength behind my swings. It still took three hits to even crack the glass and another two to finally bust through it. Shattered glass sparkled in the moonlight now streaming in from outside, and the blast of fresh air was the sweetest I'd ever smelled. I couldn't resist lowering the towel and inhaling deeply before using the hammer to knock out any remaining shards in the window frame and laying another towel across the ledge to keep us from being cut to ribbons as we crawled through.

I got down and took Charlotte's shoulders again, shaking her slightly to make sure she paid attention to me as I shouted, "I've got the window open. We need to crawl through. If I get you up there, can you do that for me?"

Her eyes looked dazed and glassy now, and I worried she'd gone into shock on me, but she had enough wherewithal to nod. Good girl.

"Okay." I climbed up on the counter, then helped her up as well. "Be careful on your hands. I got the glass off as much as I could, but it might still be sharp."

Another nod, and I boosted her up to the window. I felt her stiffen as she placed her palms on the window ledge, then saw the telltale spread of crimson on the white towel. Shit. My heart hurt, but it was better than burning to death.

She scrambled through the small opening, wiggling slightly when her hips got stuck, and then she was out. I followed close behind her, cursing up a blue streak when I cut myself too on that damned ledge. But outside I could hear Charlotte coughing and gagging, and I knew we'd be okay. That was all that mattered. After dropping down to the alley, I yanked off the towel over my mouth and rushed to her side, pulling her tight to me and holding her close.

We were alive.

At first, she hugged me back. Then her arms went slack, and I drew back to see that she'd fainted. Fuck. I bent to lay her gently on the ground, then checked her pulse and breathing. Behind me, at the end of the alley, were shouts from the fire department. Soon, searchlights and sirens filled the air.

Two EMTs rushed forward to check on me and Charlotte, but all I could see was her pale face as she sprawled on the ground, looking for all the world like she was dead. I knew she wasn't. Had felt her pulse flutter against my fingertips. Had seen the rise and fall of her chest. But in all my years as a SEAL, on all those missions in the worst of the worst parts of the world, fighting the most hellacious battles, I'd never been as shaken as I was at that moment.

"You can ride along if you want," one of the EMTs said to me a short time later as I watched Charlotte's stretcher being loaded into the back of an ambulance. "If you agree to get checked out too."

"Fine." I didn't hesitate, though I felt okay. No broken bones, no permanent damage. Just some cuts and bruises. But I would've agreed to walk across a field of spikes barefoot if it meant staying with Charlotte. Of course, the guy looked me over, then declared what I already knew: I was okay. I climbed into the back of the rig and took a seat next to Charlotte's stretcher while a second paramedic gave her oxygen. I held her hand, grateful for the warmth of her touch.

By the time we got to the hospital, she was awake again. They wheeled us into the ER, and we sat in an exam room while the nurses and techs checked her vitals and hooked her up to more monitors to check her oxygen stats.

"What happened?" she asked me during a break in the action, her voice croaking like a bullfrog because of the smoke. "I remember climbing out the window and hugging you, then... nothing."

I kissed her hand, then held it close. "You passed out. Probably from all the adrenaline and the shock."

"The tavern?"

Her words cracked, and my heart broke. I swallowed hard, my own throat achy from the fire. "I… don't know yet. There was a lot of smoke damage, and those flames were vicious. The fire department is still there, working, but I'm not sure what they'll be able to save."

Tears rolled down her cheeks, and I felt gutted. I wanted to make it all better for her but knew I couldn't. "I'm glad you were there with me," she said, low and rough. "You saved me, Gabe."

Now my eyes stung. I wanted to tell her that she'd saved me, too, but the words wouldn't come. So I just shook my head, then leaned in to kiss her forehead, glad she was okay. We stayed like that for a while, until more nurses and techs came in to check on her.

"You need to get Savannah from my mom's," she said to me in between blood pressure checks and a quick blood draw. "I don't want the baby left without us overnight."

Much as I hated to leave her side, I agreed. The ER doc came in then, and I took that as my sign to go. "I'll get Savannah, then, and be back shortly."

TWENTY

They released me from the hospital the next day. Apparently, I'd inhaled more smoke than I'd realized when I'd panicked in the tavern kitchen. Thankfully, the doctors said there was no permanent damage done to my lungs, though I'd have to go in for regular rechecks for the next several months to be sure.

They'd bandaged up my hands where the window had cut them, but thankfully the wounds were superficial and didn't even need stitches. They also didn't cause issues taking care of Savannah, which was good too.

There was no way the tavern had survived that mess of a fire. I'd asked Gabe several times how bad it was, but he'd kind of blown me off in the hospital, giving me vague answers or suddenly needing to run to the bathroom or the vending machine.

Well, today I was going to see for myself. I had to. That bar was my life, my livelihood. And no matter what shape it was in, I needed to assess the damage and figure out a way forward. So, once I'd gotten the all clear from the doctor and the nurses had unhooked me from the monitors, I got up and got dressed, then waited for Gabe to come pick me up.

He walked in a short time later, grinning. "How are you feeling?"

"Better," I said, giving him a quick kiss, then heading for the door. "I want to see the tavern."

"Oh." He stopped. "Uh, maybe that's not such a good idea."

I turned back in the doorway to look at him. "Doesn't matter. I have to see it."

"Ms. Rhodes," a nurse said, appearing in front of me with a wheelchair, "have a seat and I'll take you downstairs."

I shook my head. "I don't need that. I just breathed in a little smoke. I'm fine."

"Hospital policy," the nurse said, not budging. "If you're admitted, you get a ride in one of these down to the exit."

"You've got no choice," Gabe said, using the nurse's arrival as another distraction to avoid what was clearly becoming a problem between us. He sidled out into the hall, then said over his shoulder as he headed for the elevators, "I'll bring the car around."

Grumbling, I plopped down into the wheelchair, feeling like an idiot. I was perfectly capable of walking myself out of this place. I was sure there were others who needed this thing more than me. Still, I didn't want to be rude to the nurse, so I sighed and tried to make small talk with her as we rode down to the first floor.

"I'm so sorry to hear about Rhodes Tavern," she said as we boarded the elevator. "My family and I used to go in there every Thursday night for the nacho special."

"Thank you," I said, forcing a smile I didn't feel, my gut cramping with tension and loss. "I'm glad to know you enjoyed it."

"Will you rebuild?" she asked as the elevator lurched into motion.

"That's the plan," I said, clutching my hands in my lap. I didn't remember a lot from after I passed out, but I did remember Gabe telling me not to worry. That the fire department had notified my insurance company. Now all I had to do was wait for an adjuster to contact me so we could go through the damage and put in a claim. "It'll probably take a few months," I said, trying to sound more upbeat than I felt. "But I hope to reopen before too long."

My optimism took a hit, though, once Gabe and I reached the site where Rhodes Tavern used to stand. It had taken some serious cajoling and a few heated glares, but I'd convinced him to bring me here. Now that I saw what little was left of my beloved bar, I felt the panic and fear from the night before rush back in nauseating waves. I realized I was gripping the dashboard so tightly my knuckles were white.

Gabe reached over and placed his hand atop mine. "We don't have to do this now. Let me take you home."

"No." I pulled away and climbed out of the car. My knees shook, whether from the shock of seeing the carnage or from what I'd gone through the night before, it was hard to say. Leaning on the car at first, I made my way around to stand on the sidewalk. Lips numb, I mumbled, "I need to do this now."

I knew waiting would only make it worse, and it was so bad already. I inhaled, squashing down the urge to cough again, and blinked at the ruins in front of me. Luckily, I supposed, Rhodes Tavern had been a freestanding structure on a corner lot, so no other buildings were damaged.

Still, from the look of things, it was a complete loss. Wisps of black vapor still rose from piles of debris, and the remnants of tables and booths stood like charred, ashy monoliths in the otherwise empty

153

space. Like a zombie, I wandered the area, careful not to step on anything that was sharp, barely aware of Gabe behind me. He hadn't said anything since we'd left the car, but I appreciated his steady strength.

"It's gone," I whispered, looking around at what had been my life. "It's all gone."

"I'm so sorry," he said, taking my hand. "I'm so, so sorry."

Suddenly, it was all too much. I turned to him, sobbing against his shoulder as it all came bursting out—the loss, the sorrow, the anger, the frustration, the love. He held me, stroking my back and whispering into my hair as we stood in the center of my burned-out bar, the world a pile of still-smoking rubble around us. Finally, when I had nothing more to give, I eased away from him and swiped the back of a shaky hand across my salt-stung cheeks. "God, I loved this place."

"I know," he said, squeezing my hand. "But it'll be okay. No matter what happens."

Sniffling, I gave a curt nod. It would be okay, because it had to be okay. I didn't only have myself to think about anymore. I had Savannah too. She was my responsibility now, just as much as Gabe's. When he left, I'd be her legal guardian, and while he'd provide financial support, I'd be doing all the hands-on parenting while he was gone.

It would take a lot of time and effort, which I was happy to do, but it also meant I needed to get this place back in operation as quickly as possible. "They'll have to demo all this and clear it out before we can rebuild," I said, looking around before moving forward again to where the actual bar had been. There was nothing left there except a hulking piece of blackened wood. I bent down to pick through the piles of ash near the base and discovered one of the old metal taps. I stifled a sob as I picked it up, and I kept digging. I found another, then another. It wasn't much, but it was something. Something of the past to take into the future, whatever it might hold.

Straightening, I held out my hand for Gabe to see. He frowned down at the slightly twisted objects. "What the hell are those?"

"Taps." I smiled. "I'm going to keep them."

"Why?" He scrunched his nose, obviously not seeing the significance I did.

"As a reminder of what's left." I gripped them tighter, my determination growing stronger. "I'll have them made into a memorial to the original Rhodes Tavern, a symbol that good things can come out of bad."

Gabe shook his head, then leaned in and kissed me, slow and sweet. "You're amazing, you know that? Even after all that happened last night, you're still the most resilient woman I've ever known."

We spent another hour or so picking through the debris, searching for clues or anything I might be able to salvage. There wasn't much. I did manage to snap some pictures for the insurance company, which was good. I was just about finished when Gabe's phone rang, and he stepped away to answer. I glanced at him, watching as his handsome face shifted from strained to relieved in about two seconds flat. Whoever was on the line must've had good news. About damned time.

Once he hung up, I waited, heart in my throat with anticipation as he walked over to me.

"That was Police Chief Wharton," Gabe said, smiling. "They picked up Elijah Harris."

Oh God.

For a second, I couldn't respond. Then I found myself smiling, too, relief washing over me despite the mess at my feet. At last, something was going right. I held on to the burned edge of the bar to keep from collapsing as the tension oozed out of my body. "Where? How?"

Gabe leaned an elbow on the bar. It was surprisingly sturdy, despite what it had been through. Kind of like the man himself. "Wharton said that while the fire gutted this place, it left the back wall largely untouched." He pointed to it. "The CSI team was able to lift a print from the two-by-four used to block the back exit door, and it matched Harris's." At my frown, he added, "Harris had to get printed when he applied to become a police officer. I'm guessing he thought the board would be destroyed in the fire, so he didn't bother wiping it down. But lucky for us, it survived."

"Wow." I took all that in for a moment. "So they've arrested him?"

"Yep. Wharton said they're bringing him up on a bunch of preliminary charges, including assault and arson, pending the results of the investigation here. Given the maximum sentences for each of those and the evidence they found last night, Wharton doubts he'll walk away any time soon."

I was shaking again, but this time from joy. The bastard had been caught. My happiness was short-lived, however, as another thought popped into my brain. "What about Alexis? Will they charge him with her murder too?"

"I'm not sure about that." Gabe frowned down at his phone. "Wharton said those charges would be tougher to prove. He said they'll keep working on it, but without something tying him to her death—more than the circumstantial stuff we presented—it'll be harder to convict him for that." He took a deep breath, then looked up at me again. "But even if they can never officially get him for killing her, Wharton said they'll do everything they can to make sure the prosecutor nails Elijah Harris's ass to the wall for what he's done."

I blinked at him a minute, letting it all sink in. The murder. The fire. The break-in. The attack in the car. The fact that even though all this was horrible, it had also brought Gabe and Savannah into my life. Finally, I whispered, "It's over."

Gabe's smile grew as he stepped forward and took me into his arms. "Yes. It's over."

We embraced, and I felt torn. I was so happy that Elijah Harris would get what he deserved, but in the back of my mind, sadness resurfaced. With the danger over and the custody case settled, there wasn't anything holding Gabe back from rejoining his SEAL team. And while I would never begrudge him his career, I wasn't sure what I'd do without him once he was gone, even temporarily.

TWENTY-ONE

The following week, I was back at the lot where the tavern had been, alone this time. The fire department had finished up, and the arson investigators had cordoned off several sections for evidence.

I checked my watch for the umpteenth time, wondering where the hell the insurance adjuster was. They'd offered me a settlement, but the amount was much lower than I'd expected and I'd asked them to reconsider their decision.

I'd updated my coverage the previous year, and I wasn't paying that extra money for nothing. So they were sending someone out again to take another look. He was ten minutes late already. Gabe and Savannah were waiting at home for me, packing for a trip to the National Aquarium in Baltimore. It was a last-minute trip, something we thought might be fun and a way to relax after the stress of the last few weeks.

After a small eternity, a white sedan with my insurance company's logo on the door pulled up to the curb and a portly man in his midfifties got out. He walked over and held out his hand to me.

"Walter Murphy. So sorry I'm late. Got caught in a meeting with my superiors and just now got away."

We shook hands, then took a quick tour of the burned-out building. I showed him the pictures I'd taken the morning after the fire on my phone, and we went over the preliminary reports from the fire department.

"Let me start off by extending our condolences for the loss of your business," Walter said, scratching his head as he stared at the area that had once been the kitchen. "This is such a shame. I'm so sorry this happened to you."

"Thanks." I inhaled deeply, summoning all my patience, and tried to lighten the mood with a bit of humor. "It's awful, no doubt about it. Zero stars. Do not recommend."

He snorted, scribbling something down on the pad of paper he had with him. He was old school, he'd said. It helped him remember details better. I honestly didn't care if he carved notes on stone tablets as long as we moved things along and I got my insurance check in a timely manner. "You know, I used to come in here on Tuesday nights. Man, those chicken wings you served were a thing of beauty."

Walter wore such an expression of ecstasy, I had to choke back a laugh. "Yes, thanks. Those were really popular." I swallowed hard and steered the conversation back to the reason we were here. "So, how are things looking, settlement-wise?"

"Well, having seen the place again, Ms. Rhodes, I think we can increase the amount," he said, and it felt like a heavy burden lifted off my shoulders. "In fact, I was meeting with my superiors earlier about your claim, and between that and what I'm seeing right now, I'm authorized to approve the full $500,000, your policy maximum."

That was… My ears rang slightly as my mind raced. It was better than the first offer, but it wouldn't be enough to cover everything. Not by a long shot. Not with cleanup and construction and all-new equipment and furniture and supplies. Not to mention food and beverage orders from my wholesale partners and the taxes that were coming due soon and payroll to keep my displaced employees taken care of in the interim and...

Fuck.

It was a good thing I'd increased my coverage, but apparently I should have gone with a higher limit. I leaned a shoulder against one of the charred walls and put my head in my hands. If only I hadn't blown off that franchising deal, I might not have been in this position.

But now... Well, now there was no franchising deal and never would be, because who the hell would want to franchise a burned-out shell of a building? Nobody, that's who. Shit.

I scrubbed my face and stared down the decision before me. Try to raise the additional funds somewhere else, or... move on.

Except this tavern was all I'd ever known, work-wise. It was my life. If I didn't have it, what else was there?

And how would I be able to care for Savannah without a source of steady income?

"I know it's a lot to take in," Walter said, patting my shoulder. Hell, I'd forgotten he was even there. "I'll put in the requisition for the check right now, as soon as I'm back in my car. That way you should have the money as quickly as possible. Do you have any other questions for me today?"

Thoughts whirling, I shook my head. I took the card he handed me, then watched him walk out of the ruins of my bar—my life—then get in his pristine white sedan and drive away.

In the end, I went back to my car, because what else was I going to do? Five hundred grand was what I'd be given, and it's what I'd have to work with. As I headed home, I tried to work out how exactly I could save my tavern on a fraction of what I needed.

I was still deep in thought about it all when I walked into the house a short while later. Gabe was full of excitement and adrenaline over a day out with his girls, as he called us. Savannah had picked up on his mood, squealing with joy from her playpen.

"Hey there. You ready for some fun?"

And how the hell was I supposed to stay down in the dumps with the two of them smiling at me?

Yes, my future had taken a serious turn for the shitty, but that didn't mean I needed to let it ruin the day. We'd planned this wonderful family outing at the aquarium, and we'd damned well have it, even if it killed me.

Gabe breezed by, dropping a quick kiss on my lips as he passed, shoving baby supplies into a diaper bag. "I booked us tickets on the train in an hour. If you're going to change, you want to do it now."

Right. I plastered on my best smile and headed down the hall to wash up and get ready, determined to have the best day ever.

It was pretty good, too, in the end.

Savannah slept all the way on the train, the gentle sway of the cars rocking her better than any chair ever could. Gabe and I sat shoulder to shoulder, holding hands and chatting about nothing in particular, just enjoying each other's company. I'd already decided not to say anything to him about the meeting with the insurance adjuster, and when he asked, I deflected, saying the money would be in my account at the end of the week and I'd start planning then.

Not a lie. Not completely, anyway.

The National Aquarium almost made me forget the challenges I was facing. There was something calming about the space, and seeing Savannah's delight filled my heart with joy. She was amazed, her little mouth hanging open in wonder as she tried to take it all in.

A couple of special exhibits were going on, and we checked out one geared toward younger children. A huge pool contained what appeared to be hundreds of stingrays swimming around, diving and swooping through the water like graceful ballerinas. Savannah squeaked and clapped with delight. Gabe carefully brought her to the edge of the tank, where you could reach in and stroke the animals' backs. At first, Savannah seemed delighted. Then she gagged loudly at the rubbery texture against her skin, making everyone around her laugh, including Gabe and me. She was such a treasure.

Next up, we visited the Jellies Invasion. "Brainless and Beautiful," the sign said, and I chuckled. "Just like some people I know."

Gabe snorted. "Me too."

Honestly, jellyfish had always kind of creeped me out, but seeing them floating around in huge tanks beneath the glimmering lights, all lacy and ghostlike and shimmering with colors, was enchanting. Gabe held my hand as we listened to the guide talk about the various species on display, including the Atlantic bay and Pacific sea nettles, the lion's mane jelly, and a short, squat little one called a blue blubber.

"That one's my favorite," I said, kissing Gabe's cheek. "The blue one."

"You're my favorite," he whispered back before kissing me.

We walked around some more, checking out an exhibit on Australia and another called Blacktip Reef, where sharks zoomed everywhere, before breaking for an early dinner. We walked to a nearby chain restaurant and got a table, and I started feeding Savannah while Gabe ordered our food. By the time the server brought our meals, I'd finished giving our girl her last bite of pears and apricots before putting the empty jar back into the diaper bag.

"Man, those tropical fish and corals at the Australian exhibit were amazing, weren't they?" Gabe asked as he put his napkin on his lap. "I remember going snorkeling at the Great Barrier Reef when I vacationed down there one time. It was unbelievable. I mean, seeing the fish here was great, but seeing them in the wild is something else."

"I bet," I said, smiling as I unwrapped my burger, doing my best to hide the gnarled thoughts about that damned insurance situation that still haunted my mind. We were having a lovely day. No way was I going to ruin that, especially when there was no way of knowing how much longer we'd have before Gabe left again. "It sounds wonderful."

"Oh, it is." He jammed his paper straw into his chocolate shake cup, then took a sip before reaching over to stroke Savannah's cheek. "Maybe one day I'll take my girls to see it for themselves."

I nodded and chewed my food without really tasting it, my heart thudding sickly against my rib cage. Those words should've made me so happy. I wanted them to make me happy. But I was worried. Worried about the tavern. Worried about my future. Worried about whether any of this between Gabe and me would last once he was back with his team, traveling the world, while I stayed here in little Harpers Ferry with Savannah.

"Everything okay?" Gabe asked, apparently more intuitive than I'd given him credit for.

"Of course," I lied, shoving more fries into my mouth, chewing and swallowing to buy some time. "Why wouldn't it be?"

He watched me for a second, then exhaled slowly before pulling his wallet out to settle the bill. "No idea. But I'm wondering if we should try to squeeze in one more exhibit or head to the train station early for

Savannah's sake." He checked his watch. "Our train heads back in three hours."

Savannah was sleeping again, so I slipped her into the carrier on Gabe's back before taking his hand again as we walked out of the restaurant and back toward the aquarium. It was less crowded now and a bit quieter. "I think as long as she's sleeping, we can fit in one more."

He agreed, and we started toward our final exhibit, my mind running through everything we'd just discussed.

Rebuilding had been my first choice, but maybe it wasn't worth the headache. But if I didn't rebuild, what was I going to do? Running a bar was basically my only life skill. I supposed I could work for someone else, but after being my own boss for years, that idea chafed.

Gabe leaned in and kissed my temple, giving another long look, curious yet confident, and I forced myself to concentrate on the day. Whatever happened, I'd deal with it and keep going, because that's who I was, what I did.

Talk about surviving through adaptation. Those octopuses had nothing on me.

TWENTY-TWO

I wasn't stupid. I could tell something was bothering Charlotte. Something had gone wrong somewhere, but I didn't want to push. Not after everything she'd been through. So I waited until after our great day was over and we were home safe and sound that night.

We got Savannah bathed and in bed, and then we settled on the sofa to watch some TV. I put my arm around Charlotte's shoulders and cuddled her into my side, kissing the top of her head before asking, "Want to tell me what's going on with you?"

She stiffened for a moment, and I knew she was thinking about whether to deny anything was wrong again, but then she finally relaxed against me. Or maybe collapsed would be a better description. Being strong all the time was hard work. I knew that all too well.

Charlotte sighed, resting her head on my shoulder. "I'm not sure what to do about the tavern."

"Hmm." I frowned, a bit confused, my chin atop her head. "What about it? Didn't your meeting with the insurance guy go well?"

"No. Yes." Another sigh. "I don't know. I'm probably just thinking about it too hard. Frankly, it's giving me a headache."

I tucked her a bit closer into my side and kissed her head again. "I'm sorry, sweetheart. I can't imagine how hard all this is for you."

I meant it. I'd lost my family, and that was a pain I'd always carry with me, but this was different. Losing her business, her livelihood, all the dreams she had wrapped up in that. She'd lost herself, in a way. If I'd woken up one day to find out my team was gone, I'm not sure what I'd do. I'd kind of built my whole world around that. To have it be taken away overnight would be devastating.

Part of me wanted to share those thoughts with her, but another part kept getting distracted by how good she felt at my side. I forced myself to focus on the problem at hand: how to navigate this new normal for Charlotte and still find a way that we could be together in the future.

An idea resurfaced, one that had started earlier today at the aquarium, when I'd mentioned taking her and Savannah with me to Australia next time. I'd never really considered it before, but it wasn't impossible.

In fact, some of the other guys brought their families with them a lot, and the wives and kids stayed on the bases closest to wherever we were deployed. CO Smith's family, for instance, had traveled the world with him. His kids knew five languages already. Imagine a life like that for my Savannah. My pulse kicked up a notch at the possibility that maybe I could have both my SEAL team and a family. "What if you came with me?"

Charlotte's posture went rigid again, and she pushed away to look up at me, frowning. "What?"

"What if you and Savannah came with me when I go back to my deployment? There are usually military bases close by and the housing is decent. You two can explore the culture, meet new people, see the sights while I'm working." When she didn't say anything else, I continued. My growing excitement was morphing into irritation at her lack of enthusiasm, but I forced that down. She was still hurting over her loss. She just needed time and the right nudge to get on board. "Look, your tavern is gone. And you know I'm sorry about that. But there's no going back to the way things were, so why not start new? Build a new life. Together. With me. What's holding you here in Harpers Ferry now?"

I'd expected her to at least embrace the possibility. She didn't. In fact, she pulled farther away from me, like I'd insulted her. I was well and truly baffled, because all I'd wanted to do was help.

"Uh, everything." Charlotte's expression was hardly joyful or even appreciative. In fact, she looked kind of pissed off. Shit. An ache grew around my heart, and I resisted the urge to rub the sore area with the side of my fist. She stood and began to pace the small living room. "I can't leave Harpers Ferry. This place is my home, Gabe. I have roots here. Why would I leave to chase you halfway around the world?"

"You wouldn't be chasing me, Charlotte." I sat forward, scrubbing a hand over my face. "You'd be getting a chance to see things, travel, experience life outside this small-town box you're in."

Okay. Maybe that didn't come out the way I'd intended. Fuck. I was messing this up.

I didn't want to fight about this. "I just mean that there's more out there to see and do and learn and *be* than what's here in Harpers Ferry." I pushed to my feet as well, too frustrated to sit on my ass anymore. "I don't understand why the idea of leaving upsets you so much. Yes, your mom is here, but it's not like we can't come back and visit her. Other than that, what else is there for you in this town? You don't have a load of friends, because you're working all the time. Or you were. I don't understand why you aren't excited about the possi-

169

bility of us traveling the world together, with Savannah. Think of the sights she'll see. Some of my buddies on the team have families, and they make it work. I could be a SEAL and a dad to my daughter. You could make new friends on the base. Have a whole new life."

"I don't *want* a new life, Gabe." She stopped and stared at me across the coffee table, and from the look in her eyes, I almost wished she'd kept walking. "My life is here. Even if the tavern is gone, I'm not interested in leaving. I guess you can't understand that, and I can't explain it, but I shouldn't have to. It's what I want, and that's it."

"But why? Can't you at least give me a reason? I think I deserve that." The plans I'd started to make in my head were all falling apart, and I wasn't sure why or how to fix them. Fixing things was what I did, who I was. The idea that I couldn't repair the most important relationship in my life right now was eating me up inside. Frustration squeezed my chest tight, and I dragged my hand through my hair. "Maybe I didn't say it right. Maybe I need to describe it better, but seriously. You could live anywhere, Charlotte. Even if you didn't want to be with me or live on a military base or be my wife, you could still get out of this nothing place. Why the hell would you want to stay here?"

Charlotte went stone still, never a good sign. "Because, Gabe, that's just it. This place isn't nothing to me. This place is everything. It's my home. It was your home, too, once. Don't you miss Harpers Ferry at all?"

When I didn't say anything, she shook her head. "I love this town. I love the mountains and the changing seasons. I love being close to DC and Baltimore but removed from them. I love all the nature and the national parks and the history." She sighed. "All that means something to me. I've built a life for myself here. Even if the tavern is gone. And I know being back here is painful for you, even if you're still denying that." I started to protest that I'd worked through it, but

170

she held up a hand, stopping me. "I'm sure every time you turn a corner here, it reminds you of losing your family—but I thought part of the reason you returned was to make peace with that, to put it to rest at last. I know you went to the graveyard and all, but these things take time, Gabe." Her voice trailed off, and she turned away. She walked over to the window to peer out, leaning a shoulder against the wall, her face in shadow now. "I thought it was getting better for you, Gabe. You've been getting out here, going places and talking to people you knew as a kid. I thought maybe you'd see that you could make a life here for yourself again, after you're done with the SEALs. That this town holds more than grief and memories."

Okay. This was not going the way I'd wanted at all. I knew Charlotte had deep roots in Harpers Ferry, but there was no way I was moving back here. She was right: there was too much baggage attached, and it was all still too painful. Even though I'd visited my family's resting place and paid my respects to them, there were still moments when it felt raw. With everything else going on, I couldn't deal with this too. So I did what I always did to cope these days. I grabbed my coat off the hook by the door and tugged it on. "I'm going out for a walk."

"A walk? Really?" She straightened and moved toward me, her expression hurt. "You're running again. You're not even going to stand here and fight for what you want? Grow up, Gabe."

"I am grown. And I've done more than enough fighting in my life to know when a battle is hopeless," I hissed, doing my best to keep my voice down so as not to wake Savannah. "It's clear to me that this conversation is going nowhere. I was trying not to make this a 'my life choices versus your life choices' kind of thing, but you took it there. And clearly that's how you see it, so..." I turned away and opened the door, needing some time and space and fresh air. The black hole I'd been trying to avoid now yawned open inside me, sucking all my happiness down into it.

"You said you know how hard it is for me to be here, but I don't really think you do," I continued. "You're right: every time I go out, someone in this town brings up my family, brings up a person I can't be anymore. I stopped being that guy when I left here at eighteen, and he's not coming back. I can't be him anymore. I... I can't, okay? I'm a different person now. I have different goals and dreams and ideas, and I can't go back, Charlotte." I sighed and hung my head. "Look. Forget I brought it up. I'm sorry. It was just an idea. I was thinking out loud, really. I don't want to fight anymore." I walked out onto the porch. "I'll be back later. Don't wait up."

TWENTY-THREE

The next twenty-four hours were about the most awkward ones of my life. Gabe and I pretended nothing had happened. We talked about the weather, about meals, about who was going to feed or change Savannah or take her for a walk, but not a word about anything important.

Not a word about our fight.

So, yeah. Not good.

For my part, I wasn't sure what else I had to say on the subject. I'd put it all out there. I loved my town, and I loved living here. And while I might have fallen for Gabe, too, harder than I'd ever thought possible in such a short time, I wasn't ready to leave Harpers Ferry behind. Sure, things were kind of a mess right now where the tavern was concerned, but I'd work through it, like I always did. I wasn't a runner. And Gabe... was.

Okay, maybe that wasn't fair. He'd been through things I couldn't even imagine. And maybe in his place I'd have wanted to get the hell out too. But nothing was really solved by leaving. Not when the truth and answers you needed were left behind.

I was still mulling all this over as I kissed a sleeping Savannah's forehead, then headed back out into the hall, closing the door silently behind me so I didn't wake her. I could hear the low murmur of Gabe's voice as he spoke on the phone in the living room. From his tone, I suspected he was on a work call. I didn't want to eavesdrop, but I needed something from the kitchen and it was my house, so…

When I reached the kitchen, with its open doorway to the living room, my heart sank. It was a work call, all right. Gabe was on the phone with his commanding officer. I fiddled around at the counter, fixing myself a cup of coffee, then rearranging the plates in the dishwasher before starting it, pretending I couldn't hear what was plainly echoing all around me.

"Yes, sir," Gabe said at last. "I'll call you by the end of the day tomorrow about my return. Goodbye, sir."

My shoulders tensed at the sound of his deep sigh, my stomach threatening to return the dinner we ate earlier. Then the sofa creaked as he got up, and his footsteps moved closer to where I stood near the sink, stopping behind me. He wasn't close enough for me to feel his body heat, but my skin tingled just the same. As it always did in his company. Old habits died hard. I kept my head down, though I could see our reflections in the dark glass of the window in front of me. I should have expected this. With Elijah Harris behind bars and Savannah settled here with me, there was nothing holding Gabe here, nothing to keep him from going back to his SEAL team.

"That was my CO," he said, confirming what I already knew. Dread bubbled like sludge in my veins. *Don't say it. Don't say it.* "They want me back on mission as soon as possible."

"Oh," I managed to force out. *Keep it together. Be supportive.* I really wanted to do both of those things, but dammit, I hated this so much. It was bringing up a bunch of shit that I hadn't thought about in a long, long time. I squeezed my eyes shut, took a deep breath, and then turned to face him, rubbing my arms against the sudden chill in my blood. "Did I ever tell you about when my dad left?"

Gabe blinked at me, then shook his head, uncertainty shining in his eyes.

"I guess I should clarify by saying when he left for the last time, since he did it so often." I managed a joyless laugh, trying to be funny even though there was nothing funny about it. Not at all. The memories flowed through me again after so many years of tamping them down and pretending everything was fine. Like tiny razors, they cut me deep. "One night when I was seven, I went to bed. He was there then, but when I woke up, he was gone. I never saw him again. Not one word in twenty years." Throat tight, I swallowed hard and battled the anger and hurt and betrayal threatening to overwhelm me. This situation was different. I knew that. And yet it seemed all too similar. Gabe was leaving Savannah, like my father left me. Like every other man in my life had always left me. As if I wasn't important, wasn't worth staying for.

I was sick of it.

"I think it's great that you're getting on with your life, Gabe," I said, my tone sharp. "Really. And I'm sure your team is eager to have you back."

He gave me a wary look. The kind animal keepers got around dangerous, spooked predators. "Look, Charlotte, I—"

"You what?" I shoved away from the counter, taking a step toward him, my face hot. "You're going to walk out on your daughter when she's just found you?"

"Hey." He frowned, holding his hands up in front of him like a shield. "That's not fair."

"Fuck fair." My rage-filled words rang off the kitchen walls, and I winced. Shit. Pissed as I was, I didn't want to wake Savannah.

Gabe tried again to reason with me. "You knew what my life was like, Charlotte. You knew eventually I'd need to go back to my team." He inhaled deeply. "But it's not forever, okay? I'll keep in touch with both of you, I promise. And I get thirty days of leave a year, so I can come back here to visit. Or I can fly Savannah out for visits, if she wants to come and if it's safe for her to be there. We'll work it out."

I had to admit that the comparison to Charlotte's father had thrown me at first. But the longer I thought about it, the more it pissed me off. I was leaving because I was doing something important: I was defending my country, not running away to avoid my responsibilities.

Jaw tight, I tried to keep my temper in check when it became clear that she wasn't going to back down from what she'd said, despite my offers and pleas. "Look, I can see that you're upset and that this is bringing up a lot of baggage for you, Charlotte, but I'm not your dad. I'm not walking away because I'm an addict or a loser or a piece-of-shit liar. I'm going overseas because I have a duty to my country and my team. I gave an oath to serve and protect when I enlisted, and I intend to fulfill it."

"I see." Her cheeks were flushed, and her eyes flashed with fury. What she lacked in size, she more than made up for in attitude, and it was one of the things I loved most about her.

Wait. What?

No. No, no, no.

I didn't love Charlotte. I didn't love anyone except Savannah. I'd learned that lesson a long time ago. People you loved left you. People you loved died. I refused to open my heart up to that kind of agony ever again.

"And do you think any of that matters to your daughter?" Charlotte asked, and it took a second for the question to cut through the sudden flurry of panic in my brain and for me to connect the dots back to our argument. She moved closer to me, her scent and heat swirling the chaos inside me to new heights. I wanted her so badly I hurt. I yearned for her, but I wouldn't have her. Not again. Not until things were crystal clear between us. This was a short-term, fling-type situation. We'd come together during a time of crisis for both of us. This wasn't love. It wasn't permanent, wasn't forever. It couldn't be. Still, my traitorous body tingled and burned for her. She poked me in the chest with her index finger, jarring me back to reality. "I can tell you from firsthand experience that it doesn't. It doesn't matter why you're leaving, just that you're gone. Savannah will still miss out on that time with you."

Then she threw her hands up and turned away, stalking out of the kitchen and into the living room. "I can't do this. Not anymore." Her hair, which she'd piled atop her head in a messy bun, had started to come loose, and a strand hung down near her cheek, bobbing and swaying with every shake of her head. I felt a wild urge to walk over and tuck it behind her ear. My fingertips burned with the desire to touch her, but I forced it down deep, clenching my fists and grinding my teeth until they ached. Charlotte stopped, the couch a barrier between us, and gave me a flat stare. "I can't give my heart to someone who's going to spend months on end, or maybe even years, overseas. I can't." She took a deep breath. "So... we can be friends, Gabe. We can even coparent Savannah, if that's what you want. But the rest of our relationship is over."

My brain was still stuck on the fact that she'd been thinking about giving her heart to me. My own chest squeezed tight at the thought. In that moment, I wanted nothing more than to drop to my knees and beg her to forgive me. For what, I wasn't sure, but if it got us back to where we'd been before, I'd do it. But then the rest of her words registered, and that moment passed, something precious and perfect dying along with it.

I hated this. Hated being forced to feel like the bad guy when I'd been up front and honest about my intentions the entire time I'd been here. And yes, things had changed. Some things, anyway. But others hadn't. I couldn't turn my back on the commitments I'd made, even if the US government wouldn't have had something to say about it. I wasn't built that way. My honor meant something to me, and I wouldn't throw it away over emotions that could be taken away without warning, leaving you alone and bereft and without any purpose or direction in life.

I had direction now. I had purpose, thanks to my team. They were as much my family now as the one I'd lost. And I owed them my life. Because without them, I was damned sure I wouldn't be here now.

Which meant it was time to leave. I couldn't stay here any longer. Not after everything that had happened. I'd done what I'd come to do and more. I'd made peace with my family's deaths. I'd visited their graves. I'd spent time in my hometown. I'd helped put the police on the track of Alexis Barnes's murderer, and I'd found and claimed my daughter. I loved Savannah, more than I'd ever have thought possible.

In these few short weeks, she'd become part of my heart, my soul. But she was young, too young to even remember what happened right now. I'd go back to my team and finish out this enlistment. Then I'd figure out what to do from there. I'd come back for visits, like I'd told Charlotte. I'd made progress here, and I didn't want to lose that. But Harpers Ferry wasn't my home anymore. Hadn't been for a long time.

Honestly, I didn't need a home.

And yeah, maybe I wasn't as keen to go out on another mission right now as I usually was, but I'd get over it. The timing sucked, sure. Each time I closed my eyes, all I could see was Charlotte and Savannah and how happy we'd been together these past few weeks... but that wasn't reality.

Reality was, I'd signed on to be a SEAL and I had obligations to keep. How I felt or what I thought about it didn't matter. Forget the stabbing pain in my heart. Forget the crushing weight of knowing the minute I walked out that door, I'd ruin any chance that Charlotte and I might somehow find a happy future together. She expected me to walk away, because that's what she knew. I expected her to let me go, because that's what people do. They disappear.

And where did that leave us?

Nowhere.

I sucked in some much-needed oxygen, then gave a curt nod. She probably expected to me to continue fighting about this, but I was done. There was nothing left to fight for anyway, right?

"Fine," I said, heading down the hall to the guest room, hoping she'd stop me but knowing she wouldn't. It was too late to stop any of this now, and I was too tired to try. "I'll pack up my stuff and move out tonight."

TWENTY-FOUR

I moved into a hotel room in Harpers Ferry, close enough to walk to Charlotte's to be with Savannah, but far enough away that it gave me some much-needed space to work out the tangle of tension I now found myself in. After a few days, though, the short distance wasn't enough. I felt trapped in my head, and this weird suffocating feeling lingered in my chest. I needed out for a while.

So, the next morning, I called Charlotte to make sure she didn't have anything important on her schedule that day, then asked if she minded if I got away for a bit. She said no. It was the most we'd spoken since our fight.

An hour later, I was on a train heading into DC. I'd phoned my friend Matt and asked if I could visit. I wanted to thank him in person for his help in capturing Elijah Harris. And, truthfully, I'd been thinking a lot about the security business he'd started. I was curious about it, how it worked for a retired SEAL back in the real world.

The constant sway and bump of the train was soothing, and between checking my emails on my phone and dozing a bit, it seemed like I was there in no time. I grabbed a taxi and rode to the address Matt had given me, paying the driver and stepping out on the curb in front of a modest, glass-covered building. It seemed like kind of an odd location for a security company, seeing as how all that glass wasn't exactly private or secure. I walked inside to a reception desk where a woman was working.

She looked up from her computer and smiled. "How may I help you?"

"Hi, I'm here to see Matt Ryeland, please," I said, smiling back. "He's expecting me."

"Sure." She took my name, then made a call before pointing to a small waiting area in the corner. "Have a seat. He'll be right with you."

"Thanks."

Sure enough, I'd barely sat my butt in the seat before a door opened down a short hallway and Matt came out, grinning from ear to ear and looking pretty much the same as the last time we'd seen each other— still tall, still muscled, still all long limbs and a piercing stare. We shook hands, then exchanged a quick bro hug before he stepped back, hands on hips.

"It's been too long, dude," Matt said, laughing. "You still look the same."

"You too." I grinned. "So, you going to show me around, or what?"

"Sure." He gestured for me to follow him down the hall. "To what do I owe the honor today?"

I shrugged. "Just need a bit of a break. Thought I'd see in person what you're up to, since I'm close by."

For now.

"Cool." We stopped in front of the elevators, and he pushed the Down button. We chatted about our history and our lives since we'd last seen each other, and when the car arrived we rode down to what I assumed was a storage basement. I was telling him all about Savannah when the doors slid open to what looked like some kind of action movie secret training facility.

"Holy shit," I said, unable to keep the awe from my voice. I'd been wrong about this place not being right for a security office. It was like security nirvana down here. He took my stunned silence in stride and showed me around the training rooms and target range and even what looked like an interrogation room, though Matt said it was a meeting space. Uh-huh. Sure. There was also a workout room with a full set of weight machines, top-of-the-line treadmills, a boxing ring, and heavy bags.

"There's a more formal conference room upstairs, near my office, for meeting business clients," Matt said when we stood near the elevators once more. "You know you've got a job here if you want it, when you're ready to retire, dude. We're teammates. I'll hire any and all of you to work here."

"Right." I wasn't sure what to say to that, so I simply nodded.

But Matt apparently wasn't ready to let it go. He kept pressing. "You've been in for ten years now, dude. And if you're lucky you can go for another ten. But then what? What do you do after that? Take a desk job at the Pentagon?"

"I don't know." My feelings about all this were still too raw after the other night, and I didn't want to get into it today, no matter how grateful I was to Matt for his help. "It's not something I want to think about right now, okay?" I snapped, sounding harsher than I'd intended.

Matt snorted, his gaze narrowed like he saw right through my bullshit. "Hey, I'm just trying to help you out, man. We all have to think about it someday. Every SEAL gets there." The elevator doors opened, and we climbed aboard to ride back up to the first floor. Matt raised a shoulder. "Figured since you'd walked into a ready-made family, maybe you were getting to the point where you're asking yourself these kinds of questions. I know I did."

That earned him some serious side-eye from me.

He chuckled, then shook his head. "Fine. I met a woman. When I came home on leave. That's where it started for me." His grin grew wider by the second. "Now we have a son and daughter on the way."

"Twins?" I asked, my eyes widening.

"Yep."

"Wow." I wanted to be happy for him. I *was* happy for him. But I was also sad and upset for myself, because of Savannah and the thought that I'd be leaving her soon. "Great news. Congratulations."

The words sounded flat to my own ears.

If Matt noticed, however, he didn't mention it. He held the elevator doors for me to get off, then followed me out into the hall before leading me to his office. It was a bit cluttered, but then that was Matt. Always five million things going on at once. The guy always seemed to balance it all, though. I was never sure how he did it.

Matt closed the door, and we sat down, him behind his desk and me in a chair in front of it. Then he cut through the shit. "So," he said, steepling his fingers in front of him. A move I remembered well from our missions together. It meant he was going in for the kill, and my stomach lurched. "Tell me why you're really here, dude. 'Cause I know you didn't come all this way just to look in a mirror."

I opened my mouth to answer, then snapped it shut again. All the emotions that had been roiling inside me since I'd first set foot back in Harpers Ferry—sadness, grief, love, loss, anger, hope—threatened to choke off my air supply. But I couldn't tell Matt about that. Not with words, anyway. It was too real and vulnerable, and I wasn't ready. So instead I asked, "How about we go back downstairs and try out that workout room?"

"You got it," Matt said, pushing to his feet again. "Come on. I've got clothes you can change into. Always keep an extra set handy, just in case."

Twenty minutes later, we were in the boxing ring, gloved up and throwing jabs and punches at each other. It had been a long time since we'd done this together, and I'd missed it. Matt and I were about the same height and build, and our skills were well matched. Meaning when I tried to get him in a headlock, he'd already anticipated it and managed to get out of it fast. Same with me. We went at it for a good hour or so, working up a sweat and—for me, anyway—working out some of my knotted feelings. It was fun, and I was enjoying myself… until something dark and dangerous that I'd buried deep inside rose to the surface.

One moment everything was bright and in color, and the next it went all gray and shadowed. My chest felt tight all of a sudden, and I couldn't breathe. Matt kept egging me on, throwing punches and weaving away from mine, and a red haze descended over my vision as my mind filled with everything that was wrong, everything that had hurt me, everything that I'd lost or fucked up in my life.

All at once, I wasn't playing around. I was fighting for real, punching and hitting and struggling to defeat all the demons from my past and my present, fighting for my future and for a life that made sense to me again.

For his part, Matt took it in stride, letting me tire myself out before he went back on the offensive and landed me on my ass with one well-placed right hook. One second I was facing him in the ring, and the next I was flat on my back on the mats, blinking up at the ceiling while my ears rang and my jaw ached.

To say I was surprised was an understatement. In all the years I'd known him, Matt had never beaten me before. Fought me to a draw, yes, but not put me down like that. He held a hand down to me and helped me up, steadying me on my feet.

He shook his head, then spit out his mouth guard to say, "Dude, you're off your game if you're letting me win. Best get your head out of your ass and go home and fix things before it's too late."

I stood there alone while he ducked out of the ring and headed for the locker room.

Maybe he was right. Maybe I did need to go back to Harpers Ferry and deal with the mess I'd helped create there with Charlotte and Savannah. Maybe it was time to face it once and for all.

What really knocked me back a step, though, was the fact that I'd put the thoughts "home" and Harpers Ferry together.

TWENTY-FIVE

My house was too quiet without Gabe.

Which was ridiculous, because up until a few weeks ago, I'd been perfectly fine being here by myself. Now, though, I felt bored and restless, and I didn't like it one bit. Mainly because no matter what I tried to do to distract myself, my thoughts kept circling back to Gabe and the awful fight we'd had.

I got up and paced my living room, scanning for any dust balls I might have missed. Sleeping had been a problem, too, my bed feeling too large and too cold without him beside me. It scared the living shit out of me, to be honest.

What I should be doing was working on the plans to rebuild the tavern, but I was too damned upset about the fight with Gabe. Instead I was cleaning. Using my hands relaxed me. But, of course, the tavern wasn't an option now, so I was dusting and vacuuming my already spotless house.

I took a deep breath and glanced over to where Savannah was playing happily in the corner. Maybe we needed to get out for a bit. Except it was chilly and rainy, so somewhere indoors.

Which pretty much meant my mom's.

With a sigh, I walked down the hall to change out of my sweats into jeans and a cute top. Man, I was really hard up if I was willingly going to spend time in my mother's day care. I snorted and went into the bathroom to tidy my hair. I mean, it wasn't like Mom and I hated each other. Things between us were just a bit… strained sometimes. Mostly because she'd always kept pushing me to do more, be more than a bar owner in a small town—while I'd been perfectly happy being and doing exactly that.

The pushing had started back in high school, when I'd made decent grades and gotten a scholarship to the local community college. The pushing had gotten worse when I'd graduated with my bachelor's degree in business and decided to take out a small business loan and buy the tavern where I'd bartended to supplement my income through school.

She'd wanted me to move to DC, maybe get a government job or work for a politician, but that wasn't for me. I loved my small-town life and my small-town tavern. Loved seeing all the familiar faces, hearing about their lives.

At the thought of the bar and what I'd lost when it had burned, my breath caught and my knees felt wobbly. I gripped the edge of the vanity and stared at my reflection. I wished things were different. That the bar hadn't burned. That Gabe and I hadn't fought. That our future together hadn't gone off a cliff.

Shit.

I squeezed my eyes shut and shook my head. Wishing things were different didn't help. Life was as it was, and the sooner I accepted it and moved on, the better. That was the pragmatist in me talking. Unfortunately, my hopeless romantic side was still a quivering, blubbering mess and kept throwing up images of Gabe and me together in my head. The way he smiled, the sound of his laughter, the feel of his arms holding me tight, making me feel safe, making me feel invincible.

No. Enough.

Savannah squeaked in her playpen, and I forced myself to straighten, to square my shoulders and walk out of the bathroom and down the hall, head high. This was ridiculous. I wasn't the kind of person who needed a relationship to make me whole. Hell, until Gabe showed up, I'd never even thought about getting married and having a family someday. I didn't like to be tied down.

I picked up Savannah, and she threw her chubby little arms around my neck and nuzzled her face into my skin, and my chest constricted so hard and so fast I thought my heart might stop. She was so sweet, so precious, and now I couldn't imagine a future without her.

Except that's exactly what I'd need to do, because Gabe was leaving, and Savannah was his daughter.

Oh God.

With the baby squirming in my arms, I tried to tamp down the growing anxiety and anguish inside me and focus on getting to my mom's. It would be better there. Noisier. She usually had at least three or four kids she was watching, and damn, I could use the distraction of that. So I fastened Savannah into her carrier and got our things together, then locked up the house and headed out to my car.

I'd forgotten to call Mom and tell her I was coming, but hey. That's what family was for, right? Besides, I didn't think she'd mind an extra set of hands to help her with the kids.

As it turned out, Mom had three other babies that day in addition to a couple of toddlers, so she was glad to see me. The toddlers were playing in the living room, with the babies in playpens or bassinets along the walls. I got Savannah set up in her walker near the toddlers and gave her some toys, then went into the kitchen, where my mom was getting me coffee. "What else do you need help with?"

Mom glanced at me over her shoulder. "I'm not sure yet. Let me think. I'm not used to having help during the day."

"Hmm." I took my mug, holding the warm porcelain between my chilled palms, and rested on a stool at the kitchen island overlooking the living room. Savannah was gurgling and banging her toys around, having a grand old time with her new toddler friends. For the first time in what felt like forever, I smiled. This was good, coming here. I wanted to be busy. Needed to be busy to keep my ghosts at bay. I sipped my coffee, then swiveled to face my mom, who was futzing with snacks at the counter. "Well, I'm yours for as long as you want me today, so…"

"Really?" Mom looked up from the Goldfish crackers she was dividing into piles. "Nothing on your agenda today? What about Gabe?"

"Oh." Hearing his name hit harder than I expected, which was silly. It was just a name, right? The name of the most wonderful man I'd ever known. Smart and funny and kind and considerate and sincere and honest and trustworthy and— I stopped that train of thought before it careened off the rails into forbidden territory. I shrugged and tried to sound nonchalant, even though I was aching inside from missing him. "He went into DC for the day, to visit a friend."

Mom blinked at me a moment, then returned her attention to her crackers. The line between her brows was more defined now, meaning she was thinking about things. That usually meant trouble for me. She surprised me, though, by bringing up a friend of hers instead of getting on me about moving forward without the bar. "Remember my friend Gladys?"

"Sure." Considering the population of Harpers Ferry was less than three hundred, and between the bar and being a lifelong resident here I knew pretty much everyone, it would be hard for me to forget. "What about her?"

"She dyed her hair purple," Mom said, then glanced up at me, eyes twinkling.

"Seriously?" I must have been busier than I thought the past few weeks to miss something like that. "Wow. That's… interesting. Why?"

"I don't know." Mom shrugged. "She said she wanted a change. She's fifty-five, you know. Same as me."

"Yeah." Mom and Gladys had gone all through school together and been friends ever since. "Well, good for her," I said and meant it. Change was good. Inevitable. Better to accept it than battle against it. I swallowed more coffee, glad for the scalding heat on my throat because it distracted me from the lump of sadness there. "How does it look?"

"Surprisingly good!" Mom grinned now, looking up at me. "Actually, I've been thinking about doing it myself. Maybe pink, though, instead of purple, because pink's my favorite color. What do you think?" She patted her hair, the same sandy brown as mine, though hers was streaked with gray now. "I talked to my stylist about it, and she said the color takes pretty well to gray, so it would look like I have streaks of pink in my hair."

I squinted and thought about it for a minute, then grinned myself. "I think you should go for it. You only live once, right? And if you don't like it, you can cover it up or wait for it to grow out."

191

We chatted for a while about nothing in particular—the weather, the goings-on in town, my latest phone call with the insurance company about how the amount they were offering wouldn't even begin to cover the price tag to rebuild. Before my mom could respond to that last topic, though, Savannah started fussing in the living room, and I got up to tend to her.

By then it was about her lunchtime, so I scooped her up out of her walker and carried her into the kitchen with me to get her bottle ready. My mom was still standing at the island, getting the snacks and food ready for the other kids. She watched me as I fed Savannah, then finally took a deep breath and asked, "What's going on?"

Frowning, I looked over at her, then back at Savannah, trying to dodge the question. "What do you mean?"

"I mean, it's nice having you here today and all," Mom said, giving me a look. "But we both know it's not like you to come over here and volunteer to help for no reason."

Damn.

I exhaled slowly and forced my tense shoulders to relax. "It's fine. Everything's fine. I don't really want to talk about it."

"Is it the bar?" she asked, not letting it go. "Because maybe this is a blessing in disguise, honey. I mean, I know you loved that place, for reasons I've never understood. But it was tying you down. Maybe not having the money to rebuild is a sign you should be doing something else."

And there we went again.

Scowling, I set Savannah's now-empty bottle aside, then put her over my shoulder to burp her as I turned to face my mother. "It's not the bar," I snapped, probably more harshly than necessary, but dammit, what was it about mothers making you feel like you were twelve years old again with one stupid question?

She raised a brow at me. "Well, if it's not the tavern, then what is it? Because that bar has taken up all of your time for so long, and—"

Desperate not to go down that road again with her, not right now, I said the first thing that popped into my mind, which of course was, "Gabe. Okay?"

"Gabe?" she repeated, sounding surprised. "What about him?"

I took a deep breath and cradled the back of Savannah's head with my hand, loving the silky feel of her hair under my fingers. She cuddled closer to me, melting my annoyance at my mother's questions. Maybe I should talk to her about it. Lord knew she'd been through it with my father. Maybe she could put things in a different light for me. And really, what could it hurt at this point? I sighed and leaned my hips back against the edge of the counter. "He's getting deployed again."

"Oh." Mom looked sort of blank about it, and that was unexpected. I figured she'd be upset, or perhaps supportive of me because of Savannah, but nope. She acted like I'd told her he was going on vacation or something. "Where's he going this time?" she asked, putting triangles of bologna sandwiches on colorful plastic plates for the toddlers, then adding a pile of crackers to each. "How long will he be gone?"

"I don't know," I said, my shoulders slumping as Savannah gave a loud burp, then fell asleep against me. "I didn't ask."

"Why not?" There was that line between Mom's brows again, her expression concerned.

"I don't want to know. I'm not involved in that."

Mom's gaze flicked to Savannah, then back to me, her brow arching higher. Yeah, she wasn't buying that at all. "I'm pretty sure the judge would see that differently, since you're her legal guardian and all."

Crap. This conversation wasn't going the way I'd intended at all. I shook my head, then stared down at the floor, digging my stockinged toe into the hardwood. "That's just it, though, Mom. I'm her legal guardian. All that means is that while Savannah is little, she stays with me while Gabe's away. But as she gets older, she can move to military bases close to him to be with her father when he's not working. It's all temporary."

"Doesn't sound temporary to me." Mom put away the lunch supplies, then got the toddlers set up at the table to eat before walking to the sink beside me to wash her hands. After drying them, she reached up to pat my cheek. "I love you, Charlotte. More than you'll ever know. But, honey, it's time for you to stop being afraid of being left behind." I opened my mouth to argue, but she put a finger over my lips to stop me. "Or being afraid of leaving your comfort zone. Remember Dustin from high school?"

The guy I'd loved and lost because he'd gone away to England without me? Yeah, I remembered. And yes, he'd asked me to go with him, but I'd said no. I couldn't leave Mom behind to fend for herself —and I wasn't the one who'd gotten accepted to college there, anyway.

Then he'd asked me to wait for him, but really. We were both young, with our whole lives in front of us. Waiting, expecting a high school relationship to last through that kind of separation, would have been foolish. I wasn't a person who waited around for someone to come back to me. Period. End of story. At least, that's what I'd always thought.

"The thing is, honey," Mom continued, "I'm afraid that if you keep letting yourself get held back by fear, you're going to miss out on so much." She sighed. "I don't want you to end up like me, stuck in this little town, wishing for what might have been. I'm not saying Harpers Ferry isn't a great place, if that's what you want. But you should consider it carefully. When I met your father, I didn't do that. I was young and naive. He was charming and worldly and basically swept me off my feet. Rather than thinking about the long term, I acted impulsively with him. I'm not saying I regret having you. Not at all. In fact, the opposite is true. I never knew how much I wanted a daughter, how much I wanted you, until I had you. You gave my life meaning, purpose. You gave me a future." She took a deep breath. "Maybe the tavern is your big dream. Maybe Gabe is the guy for you. I'm hoping you take the time you need to make the right choice for you and your life. Please don't let the past or some guy with charm and charisma convince you to do something you don't want to do."

"What if I don't know what I want to do?" I asked.

"I think you do. Deep down. You just have to have the courage to make the choice and commit."

Commit. There was that fucking word again. God, I was so tired of hearing about commitment.

Frustrated, I turned away. Anger bubbled inside me, searing my veins. I was angry at being called out like that by my mom. Angry at my life falling apart in front of my eyes. Angry at being stuck in exactly the same spot again, having to choose between love and life.

Why couldn't I ever have both? But mostly, I was angry at myself. For not being stronger, for needing Gabe more than I needed my next breath, for fucking everything up like I always did because my fucking father abandoned me.

But I couldn't say or deal with any of that right now. It was too much. So I bailed.

"I need to go," I said, packing up Savannah and taking her home before my mom could say anything else and make me feel even worse about my crappy life choices.

TWENTY-SIX

There I was, back at the train station, trying to sort out my fucking feelings.

Loser.

The ring of Matt's voice in my head made me snort as I stared at the departures board above me. At least this time I wasn't quite so conflicted about going back to Harpers Ferry. That didn't stop me from pacing, though. I'd picked up that habit from Charlotte. One of many things I'd gotten from her that I'd carry with me forever.

Truth was, I'd been thinking about my conversation with Matt earlier. He'd given me a lot to think about, and I was only now starting to process it.

Like my career. Did I really want to lose Charlotte over being a SEAL? If you'd asked me three months ago, I'd have said yes. No-brainer: I'd rather have my career than a relationship. But now things were different. And what about Savannah? What kind of parent would I be, running off on active duty all the time? Would I be a real father to her, or just someone who drifted in and out of her life? We got sent into some of the most dangerous situations in the world. What if I didn't make it home? Then Savannah would've lost both of her biological parents. I hadn't spent a lot of time talking to the guys on my team about how they handled that situation, but I should. I needed to now. Things had changed.

I sighed. It was stupid to deny it, to pretend I could go back to my old life when it no longer fit. Not the way it had, anyway.

Shit.

Then there were my feelings about it all. As I'd told Charlotte, I'd joined the Navy at eighteen. Worked my way through training and become a SEAL. They gave me a new purpose, a new way to be. I'd never questioned it—in fact, I'd embraced it. Until now. But if I gave up that persona, who was I? What would I be then? One more veteran searching for meaning in a civilian world? The thought made me shudder. No. I knew myself well enough to know I needed a purpose, a reason to get out of bed every day. The SEALs gave me that. But maybe there were other ways to find that, too, ways I hadn't considered or explored yet.

There was also a sense of honor that came with serving my country. In some ways, it had felt like a tribute to my family, even. But now... well, perhaps now it was time to find a new way to honor their memories. And what better way than to be happy? Happy with Charlotte and Savannah and the very real possibility that I could start a new family of my own. If I hadn't blown it already.

God, what a mess.

I scrubbed my hand over my face and stared up at the arrivals and departures board again.

I loved Charlotte.

I realized that now. Loved her more than I'd allowed myself to love anyone in a long, long time. But was that enough? From the fight we'd had, maybe not. She was determined to stay in Harpers Ferry. Refused to even consider moving anywhere else with me, especially overseas. So where did that leave us? She was my daughter's legal guardian, but I wanted her to be so much more.

And Savannah. I'd never felt more protective of another human in my life. She was a part of me, the best part, and I wanted to be there for her. For all the birthdays and graduations. For the dance recitals and the homework and even the boring days where nothing much really happened. I needed to be there for it all. And I wanted Charlotte by my side during all of it. We made a good team. The best team.

"Now boarding, service to Pittsburgh, with stops in Rockville, Harpers Ferry, Martinsburg..." the overhead PA system said, continuing to list stations before concluding, "leaving Track 19 in twenty minutes."

Right. That was me. I wove through the people in Union Station, ignoring the glorious architecture around me—the soaring vaulted ceiling with its ornamented arches, the statuary, the ornate clock—as I hurried toward my gate, my boots squeaking on the gleaming marble floors. I had no idea how things were going to work out between me and Charlotte, but I knew I needed to get home to figure it out. And yeah, despite all my protests, Harpers Ferry was home.

I got to the gate and pulled out my ticket to show the conductor. Checking my watch, I fidgeted a bit. If I was lucky, I'd get back to Charlotte's house in time to help put my daughter to bed.

On board, I found a seat near the window, then stared out as the train finished boarding and we pulled out of the station. The rock and rumble of the train around me was oddly soothing, and I couldn't help thinking back to when I'd first arrived here a few weeks ago. I'd been so nervous, so uncertain. I felt none of that now. Only a realization of what I stood to lose if I didn't make the right decisions.

I'd made peace with the loss of my family. Now it was time to make peace with my future, whatever it was going to be.

Fatigue, bone-deep and drugging, swept over me as we traveled out of DC and into the countryside. I hadn't intended on napping. I'd have said I was too keyed up to sleep at that point, but somehow, next thing I knew, we were pulling into Harpers Ferry. I yawned and stretched, rubbing my eyes before peering out at the familiar depot. It wasn't even a station, really, just an old wooden ticket office with faded green paint and an overhang.

Nervous energy zinged through my body as adrenaline flooded my bloodstream. I was here. The time was now. It was the same feeling I got before a big mission, only what was on the line was so much more personal than any war or skirmish or regional conflict we'd ever handled in the SEALs. When I stepped off the train, gravel crunched beneath my boots and damp, chilly air jolted me wide awake. I was starting across the small parking lot adjacent to the ticket stall when my phone rang.

I glanced down at the screen, half expecting to see Charlotte's name there. Like maybe I'd somehow telepathically communicated how much I missed her. But no, the call was from Chief Wharton. I coughed to clear the disappointment constricting my throat, then answered as I began to walk the short distance to Charlotte's house. "Hey, Chief. What's up?"

"Elijah Harris has escaped custody."

That stopped me dead in my tracks, my stomach in free fall. "What?"

My brain froze. Stuttered. Then began to churn, processing information as Chief Wharton explained what had happened. The immediate, intense kick of even more adrenaline into my system made me shaky and light-headed. Shit, shit, shit. I needed to get home, get Charlotte and Savannah, get them to safety. *Now*. I took off at a jog, moving as fast as I could while still keeping the phone to my ear.

"We were transferring him to the county jail to await trial," Wharton said, his tone hard and urgent. "Somehow he got a knife. It's not clear whether he used his former LEO status to mislead one of the officers into assisting him, or what—that's something I'm going to be looking into, but right now we're in response mode. He attacked one of the guards, wounding him severely, then took off running in the ensuing melee. I've put out a BOLO and teams are searching, but we haven't found any trace of him yet."

"Jesus Christ." I stared at the area around me as I ran, as if Harris might appear on the street in front of me.

"We're doing everything we can," Wharton said, in full chief mode. He was clearly trying to put a good face on a complete clusterfuck. "We've got everyone available on this, looking for him nonstop, but as of now he's in the wind."

Fuck. Fear stabbed hot and deep inside me. This situation would be bad enough with an ordinary criminal. But Harris was a different case altogether. He was former law enforcement, so he knew all the tricks of the trade and could anticipate the moves before they were made. It made him even more dangerous.

As if sensing my thoughts, Chief Wharton said, "Don't worry. I sent a patrol car to Charlotte's house, and they should arrive shortly. She and your daughter will be fine. We've got them covered."

I wanted to believe that. I did. But I couldn't trust it. My parents and brother had been fine, right up until a random accident took them from me. And this situation was far more threatening than going for a drive. The mere thought of something terrible happening to Charlotte and Savannah nearly stopped my heart.

What was more, while I liked Chief Wharton, his department hadn't done much to bolster my confidence in their crime-solving abilities. They'd only investigated Harris to begin with because of evidence that Charlotte and I had provided to them. I got that they were a small force, doing the best they could with the resources they had, but there was no way in hell I was leaving the fate of the people I loved most in this world in their hands.

No. If anyone was going to keep Charlotte and Savannah safe, it was going to be me.

"Keep me posted," I said, then ended the call so I could focus. I needed to get to the house. Find out what was happening there, then set up a proper security perimeter. My service weapon was at the hotel, and I didn't want to take the time for a detour. I didn't need a gun anyway. I'd do what had to be done with my bare hands, if necessary. I'd already lost one family. I couldn't lose another one.

I was going to save my girls, no matter what it took.

TWENTY-SEVEN

"What should we have for dinner, baby girl?" I asked Savannah over my shoulder. She gurgled at me, then shoved her little fist in her mouth to gnaw on it.

Honestly, I had no appetite, but I knew I needed to get something into my stomach. It had been flip-flopping and twisting ever since I'd left my mom's. I glanced over at my phone where it was charging in the corner of the kitchen counter. I'd silenced it as soon as I'd gotten home, not wanting to see any calls or messages from my mom—or, worse, from Gabe. The situation sucked, and I needed some time to process all the thoughts and emotions that had come up after that conversation with my mom.

I loved Gabe. I could admit that now without wanting to run away and hide. But did loving him mean I had to give up everything that was important to me and start over? I'd put roots down here in Harpers Ferry, and cutting them seemed wrong.

"Well," I sighed. "Looks like frozen pizza it is."

I'd just pulled one out of the freezer and set the oven to preheat when a huge crash sounded from the back of the house. I had no idea what the hell had happened, and it took me a minute to register the heavy footsteps echoing down the hall. By then it was too late.

Elijah Harris stood in my kitchen, eyes wild and mouth sneering.

My heart stumbled, stopped, then raced forward, slamming against my rib cage like a bird trying to escape a trap. Thoughts careened through my brain, juked up on adrenaline. Grab Savannah. Run. Get the hell out of there.

Unfortunately, Elijah was blocking all my possible exits.

Thank God that I was between him and Savannah. Thank God.

Throat tight, I forced out words, thinking maybe I could stall him until I had a plan. His hands were empty, fisted at his sides, but that didn't make him any less dangerous. I'd seen the pictures Alexis had shown me. Those fists could smash bones and teeth, tear through flesh. They were weapons all on their own.

"W-what do you want?" I asked, knowing it was a stupid question, but it was all I had in that moment.

He was trying to look past me, to see Savannah. "I want my daughter."

"You can't have her."

When he laughed, I realized how pathetic I sounded. But Elijah didn't know what he was up against. He had no clue how hard I'd fight to keep that baby safe from him. His gaze flicked from me to her, and any ideas I had about concocting some elaborate plan to trap him and keep him at bay until the cops arrived—*if* they arrived, seeing as how I hadn't managed to call them yet—evaporated.

Instinct stronger than anything else I'd ever felt before took over. Primal. Fierce. Old as life itself. I yanked Savannah from her carrier and ran. By some miracle, Elijah went the opposite way around the kitchen table, dodging when I wove, which left me a slim passage to get down the hall. I ran faster than I ever had, wincing at Savannah's unhappy wail but knowing this was it: our only hope of survival.

His footsteps pounded down the hall after us, loud and fast and nearly overpowering the timpani boom of blood in my ears. With barely a second to spare, I skidded into my bedroom, bare feet squeaking on the hardwood floor, and managed to get the door closed just as he reached the threshold.

Shit. Shit, shit, shit.

Elijah body-slammed the door, and I dug in my heels, leaning back against my side of it, using all my weight and willpower to keep him out as I scrabbled to lock it.

Wham. Wham.

The wood creaked and groaned under the stress but held firm. Older houses had their shortcomings, but damn if they weren't built solid. I said a silent prayer, Savannah's head cradled against my shoulder, my hand cupping the back of her head protectively, as I tried to catch my breath.

We were safe, for the moment, but things weren't looking good. I'd left my phone in the kitchen and had never gotten around to having a landline installed. I'd never seen much point, until now. Fuck. Okay.

Think, Charlotte. Think.

Elijah's assault on the door stopped, and I relaxed a little, though I still kept a shoulder against it. Through the crack beneath the door, I could see the shadow of his feet pacing back and forth, and he was panting hard enough to hear even with the thick wood between us.

Savannah had stopped wailing, and my arms were aching from holding her so tight. I didn't want to accidentally hurt her, and I had a feeling I'd need both arms to get us out of here, so I darted over to place her in the pack and play in the corner, kissing the top of her head.

"I promise I'll keep you safe, baby girl," I whispered. "Whatever I have to do, I'll keep you safe."

I scanned the room for possible weapons, but there wasn't much to work with. Gabe had taken his gun with him when he'd moved to the hotel, so that was out. Maybe I could bust out the window and run next door for help. Yeah, that might work. I'd need towels from the bathroom, though, to cover my hands so I didn't cut myself to shreds on the shards like I did after the fire at the bar.

Oh God. The fire.

Elijah had been responsible for that too.

All at once I was back in that choking kitchen, the black smoke curling along the ceiling, the heat searing my skin. My chest squeezed and my throat constricted, my vision starting to tunnel.

I was going to have a panic attack. I *couldn't* have a panic attack. Not now. Not with Savannah's life on the line.

Hunched over, I gasped for breath and stared at a single spot on the floor until my heart rate slowed and my vision cleared. Good. All right. I was okay. At least until more pounding started on the door. The wood wasn't going to hold forever, I knew.

Gritting my teeth, I stood up, preparing myself for battle. If I tried the window escape, I'd have to leave Savannah unguarded while I got the towels and broke the glass. I couldn't risk it—my brief meltdown had wasted precious seconds.

With no other options coming to mind, I picked up an old glass perfume bottle from atop my dresser. The bottle was big and heavy and had cost a fortune when I'd bought it at a ritzy boutique in Baltimore. Weighing it in my hand, I walked back to lean against the wall beside the door. If the door opened, I could clobber Elijah on the head with it. It wouldn't take him out, probably, but it might buy me some extra time to get Savannah to safety.

I'd never have envisioned myself using a perfume bottle as a weapon or strategizing how to get a baby safely away from a murderer. Funny how the whole fight-or-flight thing sharpened your mind.

Images of Alexis flashed in my head again. I wondered if she'd fought back too.

But I couldn't think about that now. I needed to focus. "Give me strength, Alexis," I muttered under my breath, straightening, perfume bottle at the ready.

"Charlotte," Elijah said, his voice oddly calm. Like he was strolling through a garden and not beating his way into my bedroom. "Give me Savannah. She's all I want here. Just let me have her, and I'll let you live. We'll go, and you'll never hear from me again."

Like hell he was going to take my baby.

"Fuck off!" I shouted.

He growled and slammed against the door again, sounding more animal than human.

I squeezed my eyes shut and continued to barricade the door with my body as best I could. Savannah must've picked up on my desperation, because she started crying again. It broke my heart, but I couldn't leave the door unguarded to go comfort her.

"Hey, baby girl," I called, soft and sweet. "Shush. Don't cry. It's okay. Everything's okay."

The words came out blurry because of my tears. I hated that I was crying. I needed to be strong, to prepare for the battle ahead. If I was going down, I was going down swinging. I wasn't feeling sadness so much as a whirling combination of emotions. Fear, of course, but also anger and regret.

That last one was huge. I regretted fighting with my mom earlier, because I knew she only wanted the best for me, even if we differed on what that was. I regretted that if Elijah came crashing through that door, there'd be little I could do to stop him from getting to Savannah, and God only knew what that would mean for her.

But most of all, I regretted not talking to Gabe and working out the problems between us. Not telling him how much I loved him every second of every day we'd had together. Now I'd be dead, and he'd never know.

A snarl of pure frustration ripped from my lungs. Enough of this bull-shit. Elijah Harris was a killer. He'd already murdered my best friend. He'd probably do the same to me. But there was no way in hell I was going down without a fight.

I stepped away from the door at the same moment he slammed into it yet again, and this time the wood gave way in a horrific, splintering explosion. Then Elijah Harris was in front of me, teeth bared and eyes wild, glittering with menace. I put myself between him and Savannah as best I could, then swung the bottle at his head for all I was worth.

My hand connected with the side of his skull, and beneath the heavy glass I felt the bone crack as his skin broke and blood flowed into his eyes. He grabbed for me, catching my wrist and twisting hard so I dropped the bottle. I screamed and scratched, doing everything I possibly could to keep him away, but it wasn't enough.

One second I was standing in front of him, the next he had me pinned to the wall, his fingers tight around my throat as my feet dangled helplessly in the air, kicking at nothing. I wheezed, gasped, fought for breath, but no oxygen was getting in. I dug my nails into his hand. Nothing. No response. Just a dead-eyed smirk. The fucker was enjoying this.

This was how I'd die, suffocated by this asshole.

Black crept into my peripheral vision, slowly spreading, eating up the light in the room. With my last moment of consciousness, I saw Savannah, quiet now, her little eyes wide as she stared at the back of my assailant. *I'm sorry, baby girl. I'm sorry I couldn't protect you. I'm sorry I wasn't enough.*

As Elijah's grip strengthened and my vision winked out, my last thought was for Gabe.

I love you. I'm sorry...

Then, nothing.

TWENTY-EIGHT

I ran up the street toward Charlotte's house even as sirens wailed closer and the sound of tires screeching up the street signaled the imminent arrival of the police. I couldn't wait for backup. I could hear Savannah crying at the top of her little lungs inside, and that immediately kicked me into "Fuck it" mode. I ran for the front door.

If Elijah Harris had done anything to harm even a hair on Charlotte's or Savannah's head, he'd pay. I hauled off and kicked the door, but nothing happened. Fuck! I tried again.

Goddamn these old houses and their solid construction. Adrenaline and desperation made me search for another way in. Spotting a small planter on the corner of the porch, I hefted it above my head and hurled it through the living room window, then climbed in after it, not caring about the glass shards cutting my hands or tearing my clothes.

I quickly assessed the living room and kitchen before barreling down the hall toward the bedrooms. Fuck finesse. I wanted this guy to know I was coming for him. I was ready to tear him limb from limb with my bare hands if I had to, to protect the ones I loved. I heard the cops pull up outside, but I kept going. No one was taking this asshole down but me.

At the sound of my entry, Savannah's wails had increased. I prayed she was just crying like a normal kid and that Harris hadn't done anything to her. I already knew he was a sadistic asshole who enjoyed other people's pain. Reaching the end of the hall, I found the door to Charlotte's bedroom door in splinters. Harris looked genuinely shocked when I ran into Charlotte's room, like he'd been so intent on what he was doing he hadn't heard me bust my way into the house.

I surveyed the scene quickly. Savannah was wailing in her pack and play in the corner, face covered in tears and snot, but otherwise seemingly okay. Elijah Harris, looking every inch the monster he was, all teeth and terrible, cold glee, had his hand around Charlotte's neck, choking her against the wall. And Charlotte... Charlotte was eerily still under his touch, her face red and mottled, her eyes closed.

Fuck. Was I too late?

I didn't have time to check as Harris released his grip on Charlotte and she slid into a crumpled heap on the floor, motionless. Harris turned toward Savannah, and dark shadows gathered around me, that red haze descending over my vision again. My instincts were in overdrive, all the training deep in my muscle memory surging to the forefront. Above it all beat a steady stream of urgency and an unrelenting need to protect what was mine.

Elijah looked back at me, over his shoulder, his expression oddly blank. Completely devoid of emotion. I'd only seen that a few other times in my life, in the most dangerous battles I'd been in. It was the look of a man who'd broken, who'd given up the last shreds of his humanity. Who loved the kill too much.

Elijah Harris was a murderer. There was no doubt in my mind. And today, he was going to pay.

The next few minutes seemed to happen in slow motion. Harris stepped toward Savannah, and I jumped on him, punching him hard in the kidneys. He bellowed and turned to face me, lumbering forward and swinging hard.

He caught the side of my head before I could duck out of the way, ringing my bell a bit, but I managed to right myself. I felt blood trickling from my temple, but it barely registered. All I was focused on was bringing this asshole to his knees. Stopping him from hurting Charlotte and Savannah. Stopping him from hurting anyone ever again.

Behind me, I heard a feeble cough, then the sound of movement on the hardwood floor.

Charlotte.

My heart leaped in my chest.

She was alive.

Adrenaline surged through me.

We could have another shot, if I put this asshole down for good. Savannah wailed again, as if in agreement. *I got you, sweetheart.*

Daddy's here, and he's never going to let you down again.

Then Harris was on me again, and we were locked in combat. We tumbled across the floor, fighting dirty. Somewhere in the back of my mind, I heard the sickening crunch of my ribs breaking, felt the shooting pain in my side when I took a deep breath, but I couldn't stop. Wouldn't stop.

I kept whaling on Harris for all I was worth. He'd had training, too, but he was no match for my strength and fury. He did land some good punches, one on my temple that split the skin and sent blood running down my cheek and into my eye, temporarily blinding me on one side, but I kept on going after him, pummeling him anywhere and everywhere I could reach, my only objective keeping him down until the cops arrived. Chief Wharton had assured me they were on their way, but who the fuck knew anymore?

At one point, we hit a wall—literally—and Harris was kicking and screaming and clawing at me, trying to choke me like he'd choked Charlotte. In his frenzy, he got sloppy.

I struck out then, my own muscles shaking as I grabbed a thick glass bottle that had fallen on the floor and bashed it into the side of Harris's head. The second my hand connected with his skull and I felt bone give way, I knew that was it. His eyes went wide, and then he slumped forward, landing atop me with a heavy thud, out cold.

I shoved him off me and stood, kicking him in the side to make sure he was down for good, then venting my remaining fury in another kick. When he didn't react, I crawled to Charlotte's side, glad to see her eyes open. She was barely conscious, but alive and slowly coming to. Next I moved to Savannah's playpen and got her out, holding her close and soothing her as best I could in my current condition. "It's okay," I murmured. "I'm here now. Daddy's here."

Savannah hiccuped, her cries quieting at last as she looked at me, her little fist in her mouth and her lashes sticky with tears.

"I-is s-she…" Charlotte managed to whisper, her voice wrecked from the choking. Reddish-purple bruises in the shape of fingers were already forming on her pale throat, and I had the sudden urge to kick Elijah Harris all over again. She tried to sit up but fell back against the floor, too weak. "S-Savannah…"

I walked on my knees back to her side, then slumped down against the wall, my strength waning as the adrenaline burned out of my bloodstream. I sat on the floor and turned to face Charlotte so she could see the baby. A weak smile formed on her lips, and I couldn't resist bending down to kiss her softly, even though my ribs screamed in protest, my heart overflowing with love and gratitude and respect for this woman who'd risked her life to save my daughter.

Our daughter.

The wail of sirens outside grew louder, and I glanced over again at Elijah Harris's body on the floor. Blood was trickling from the side of his head where I'd bashed him good with that bottle. He still wasn't moving. I sighed with relief. Everything was going to be okay. I felt every single one of my cuts and bruises and broken bones, but it was still the best day of my life. I bent to kiss Charlotte's forehead again, whispering against her skin the words I'd waited too long to say.

"I love you."

Charlotte blinked up at me. "I love you too."

Then the EMTs rushed in, along with the police, and our moment was lost in the chaos.

TWENTY-NINE

"*O*kay!" I said as the EMT prodded my sore jaw. I wasn't a baby when it came to pain, but I didn't like to be fussed over. I tried to brush her aside to get back to Charlotte. "Seriously. I'm fine."

"Sir," the EMT said, with patience I had to admire, "it's bleeding. It's not deep, but given the area it's in, you should probably have some stitches to keep it from opening back up again." I scowled, and she sighed. "Well, at least let me put a bandage on it so you don't contaminate the crime scene any more."

"Fine." Arms crossed, I settled back against the wall and gave her a curt nod. I'd already sat through her taping up my ribs. "Just hurry."

While she worked, I kept my eyes on the cops arresting Elijah Harris. They were reading him his rights—again—as they handcuffed him. The other EMT was sticking a hasty bandage on the guy's temple where I'd punched him good. I hoped it hurt like hell. He looked up once and caught my eye, and I barely suppressed a shudder as a chill passed through me. Those cold, dead, emotionless eyes. The look of a

217

true monster. Given what he'd done, I hoped Harris spent the rest of his days rotting in a prison cell.

In another corner, an officer was keeping Savannah occupied while we waited for Charlotte's mother to arrive and pick her up. The woman was bouncing my daughter in her arms and holding one of her favorite toys, a stuffed duck, making it quack and talk to her. I was glad Savannah was too young to remember any of this later.

Charlotte had been loaded in the ambulance already, and they were going to take her to the hospital to make sure she was okay. I'd grabbed her hand as her gurney had passed, and we'd exchanged a look. I was still trying to process what it might have meant.

Pain zinged up from the cut on my cheek as the EMT dabbed more antiseptic on it, and I winced but didn't complain. Considering none of this would've happened if I'd been here with them and not off in DC getting my shit together, pain was what I deserved.

The guilt was eating me up. Guilt and grief and this godawful anxiety gnawing at my gut, telling me that even though the danger had passed, we still had a shit ton of stuff to deal with.

Fuck. Why the hell had I walked out after our fight? Dammit, the best things in life took work. It was time to reset my default. No more walking away. The SEALs had taught me that. This time I was in it until the bitter end.

The cops finished restraining Harris and led him out into the hallway. He stumbled a bit, looking less than steady on his feet, and looked my way one more time. I bit back a fuck-you smile. He didn't deserve it. Didn't deserve anything more from me or mine at all. Good riddance. The EMTs had told me I'd given him a concussion and an orbital fracture. Damned straight. The asshole was lucky I hadn't taken his head clean off.

Chief Wharton finished talking with one of his officers, then came over to me as the EMT started packing up her kit. "We'll need you to come down and give a statement, Gabe. But with everything else going on right now, I think that can wait until tomorrow morning. Get some rest tonight."

"Thanks, Chief," I said, giving the man a curt nod, my own head aching. Harris had clocked me good a couple of times. I wasn't paying much attention to that, though, seeing as Charlotte was waiting for me in the ambulance. I excused myself and walked outside, barely registering as they carted Harris away to jail. Instead, I climbed up into the back of the rig, only cringing slightly at the pull in my cracked ribs. The EMTs were outside the ambulance, talking with the cops, so we had a moment alone together. It was only the two of us back there, and I was grateful and intended to make the most of it. I took a seat beside Charlotte's gurney and grabbed her hand, kissing it before tucking it under my chin and watching her closely. Now that I'd said the words once, I couldn't seem to keep them inside.

"I love you," I blurted again, watching her expression soften. "In case you didn't believe me the first time. I love you. I love you. I love you."

She reached for me and placed her hand on my cheek, exactly where I had a constellation of cuts. I held back the wince, because I didn't want anything to interrupt what I needed to hear from her. "I love you too."

We sat for a moment, just being together, the world outside disappearing until it was only us. The harsh fluorescent lights in the rig buzzed and flickered a bit, and there was an antiseptic smell to the air. All my attention was on Charlotte, looking far too pale for my comfort against the white sheets.

Finally, she swallowed hard, frowning. Her lips moved, and I had to lean in close to hear her words. Even so, I missed the first part. "... work things out. I can get used to deployments. Eventually."

Wait. What?

I stopped her there. "No, darling." I kissed her hand again and smiled, trying to show in my eyes all the love and joy and regret and hope I was feeling. "No. I want you to know that I've already made up my mind on that front. I'm going to put in for retirement after this last mission." At her confused look, I added, "Hell, I'd retire now, if they'd let me, but the team needs me one last time. There's no guarantee the government will let me out of my contract early anyway, but at least I can try. Or maybe I can get a reassignment to a desk job. We'll see."

Charlotte blinked up at me, her eyes huge and dark in the artificial light, her expression shocked.

"Hey." I bent and kissed her again, because it felt so good, then laughed. "Seriously. Don't be so surprised. What you said the other night got me thinking. And you were right. You put down roots here. Now I think it's time I put down some of my own. So I'm all yours. If you want me." A niggle of old fear ate into my joy before I could squash it down. Now it was my turn to clear my clogged throat. After the way I'd screwed up the other night, and so many times since I'd been here, maybe things had changed. Charlotte loved me, but was that enough? I looked away. "I hope you still want me."

The ache in my chest, the yearning, threatened to take me down faster than any punch. It scared the shit out of me to say those words, to be so vulnerable, but that was what love was all about, right?

Being open, laying it all on the line. It was time to stop running. I took a deep breath. "I really do hope you still want me, Charlotte, because I'm not sure I can live without you now. I'd be lost. Savannah would be lost too. You're the glue that holds us together."

Her eyes filled, and she shook her head. "No," she croaked. "I don't want you to do that for me, Gabe. You love being a SEAL." She paused and swallowed hard, which must have been painful, judging by her wince. "You'll resent me for it. If we're going to be together, we should both sacrifice."

"What?" I was the one surprised now. "It's no sacrifice. I'm ready. Ready to retire and start the next phase of my life with you and Charlotte. It's time." At her incredulous stare, I said, "Okay. Fine. If you'd asked me months ago, or I guess even a week ago, my answer would have been different. But that's just it. Things are different now. I'm different now, because of you. So, yeah. I'm ready to start a new phase in my life. Wherever you want to be. We can stay here in Harpers Ferry and rebuild the tavern, if you want, and be a real family." I squeezed her hand and held her gaze. "And that's something I'll never regret or resent. Not in a million years. Or we can still be a family and move somewhere else, somewhere new for both of us. Once this last deployment is over, the sky's the limit for us."

She still didn't seem completely convinced. I wanted her to know, needed her to know, how true this was for me. "Look. You were correct the other night. I went into the SEALs because my family had disappeared in the blink of an eye. And I love the guys on my team. They're like brothers to me and always will be. But now I have a new family, and I want to do what's best for them. What's best for us. Okay?"

Finally, Charlotte smiled, her eyes wet and warm with love. "Okay."

"Okay." I bent for another kiss as the EMTs climbed on board.

"Ready to head to the hospital, folks?" the EMT who'd worked on me asked before hooking Charlotte up to a blood pressure monitor and checking her pulse. "ETA five minutes."

"Ready," Charlotte croaked, squeezing my hand.

The cop who'd been watching Savannah handed her to me through the back doors of the rig, then shut us in. Soon we were rumbling down the road, Savannah gurgling and gnawing on the bill of her duck, Charlotte lying still while the EMT examined her, and me holding my daughter in my arms and feeling like I'd just gone ten rounds with Ali. We were all bruised and battered and still beautiful in our own way.

It wasn't quite the romantic reunion I'd pictured, but then life was weird that way.

Weird and wonderful and so very worth it, and I wouldn't change it for anything.

THIRTY

Six months later...

I set my tub of dirty dishes atop the bar and grinned, looking around at the packed house. I was even more proud of Rhodes Tavern than I'd been the first time around, if that was possible.

It had taken me six months to rebuild what I'd lost in the fire. Using the payout from the insurance company, plus funds from a GoFundMe page we started for donations, there was enough to get the place up and running again. There'd been plenty of days—and sleepless nights —when I was sure it wasn't going to happen, but here we were! It was real, and it felt great.

I'd opened the doors hours earlier to find a crowd waiting to get in, my bartenders and wait staff eager to get back to work and serve the lovely people of Harpers Ferry—and beyond—the best food and drink in Jefferson County. The kitchen had been hopping from the start, and now that we were nearing closing time, the cooks were still putting out hot apps and sandwiches for our guests.

But all good things had to come to an end, and after a sigh, I whistled to get everyone's attention, then announced the call for final orders. A collective groan issued from the crowd, and I laughed. "Hey, y'all can come back tomorrow night, too, remember."

People cheered and clapped, and one of my bartenders called out, "Speech!"

Damn. I didn't want to rush the end of what had been an awesome night. I'd never had a shift run so smoothly, truth be told... but I also needed to get home to relieve my mom, who was babysitting Savannah.

Soon, though, the word became a chant, until the new walls of the tavern practically reverberated with the word. "Speech! Speech! Speech!"

Okay. Fine. It seemed I didn't have a choice. I climbed atop a nearby stool and took the glass of champagne one of the bartenders handed me, then raised it in a toast. "Thank you all so much for coming tonight and showing us your support. As most of you know, the Rhodes Tavern means the world to me, and I'm so glad my community showed up after six months of our doors being shuttered." I waited for the cheers and applause to die down before continuing. "And a huge thank-you also to my wonderful kitchen staff, bartenders, and wait staff for all their hard work and patience tonight and all through this difficult time. I couldn't do it without each and every one of you. Thank you!"

More applause and cheers rang out. I drained my glass, the bubbles tickling my nose, then started to climb down—but froze when I saw a familiar form in the crowd.

It wasn't possible. But there he was.

Gabe.

He stood near the end of the bar, still wearing his fatigues and looking bone tired but happy. I jumped off the stool and ran to him, the crowd parting to let me pass. I launched myself into his arms, savoring the warmth and feel of him against my skin.

Six months he'd been gone. Six long months. I hadn't been expecting him for a few more days, though. I buried my face in his neck and greedily inhaled his scent—soap and sweat and something indefinably him.

Our lips met, and I kissed him more deeply than I should've, given that everyone in the room was watching us. Someone started clapping, and I could feel Gabe smile against my mouth. It took all my strength to pull back to meet his gaze. "What's going on? What are you doing here so early? We've missed you like anything."

"I missed you too," he said, flashing me a crooked smile that made my heart ache and my knees wobble. "The mission went faster than anticipated, and my CO released me early."

I bit my lip, afraid to say the words for fear I'd jinx it. "So you're done then? For good?"

His smile grew into a full-blown grin. "Yep. I'm done. I'm home for good."

We hugged again, this time to more applause and cheers from the crowd. I couldn't seem to let him go. I'd spent so many months wishing for him to be there, and now he was, and it was amazing. I wanted to laugh and cry at the same time from all the happiness shimmering inside me. We kissed and then kissed some more.

When he finally let go of me, people swarmed around him, slapping him on the back and welcoming him home. He took the good wishes in stride, bobbing his head politely but never taking his eyes off me. He finally untangled himself from the crowd and pulled me to a more secluded corner.

I cupped his cheeks, running my thumbs over the shadow of stubble on his jaw, by the spot where there was still a faint scar from his battle with Elijah Harris. I wondered if he'd always have the reminder of his struggle to keep us safe. I kissed him once more, just because I could, then asked, "When do you start your new job at Matt's security firm?"

"Well…" He shrugged, his firm chest brushing against my long-neglected breasts and causing a whole different kind of warmth to ignite inside me. "I didn't actually tell him I was coming home early, so…" He picked me up and grinned even wider, if that was possible. "I've got a few extra days before I start my new boring nine-to-five."

It took a moment for that to sink in past the growing want inside me, but once it did, I was grinning too. "Okay. First off, I think we both know your new job is going to be anything but boring. And second, I can't wait to have some time with you to myself, mister."

Gabe's expression shifted. He didn't say anything as he pulled me toward the door, then outside into the moonlight. We were alone in the parking lot, since no one seemed to be ready to leave the bar.

"Hey, I want you, but I'm not into exhibitionism," I said, tripping along behind him. "Especially not at my job."

Gabe smiled and looked at me but didn't say anything, and a shiver ran through me at the intensity in his eyes. We came to a stop, and he turned to face me, taking both of my hands in his.

"What's… what's going on?" I asked, looking around in confusion.

"I wanted to get you alone, so I could have your full attention."

"Well, you've got it." I laughed nervously. He was acting weird. "But why?"

"I need to tell you something."

I shivered again. What now?

Gabe cleared his throat.

"I haven't had a home in forever," he started in a low voice. "Harpers Ferry used to be my home, but that changed when I lost my family. I learned to love the road, and after a while it became my way of life. But then…" He cleared his throat again. "Then I met you. And you showed me that home isn't a place, it's a *feeling*. It's a feeling of connection, of giving yourself over to someone completely, even if it scares the shit out of you."

I smiled at that, despite the tears pooling in my eyes. He tightened his grip on my hands.

"I never imagined myself with a family, but once again, you showed me what was possible. That I didn't need to be afraid of the depth of the love I felt. I learned that loving others could free me from some of the ghosts that held me back. I spent too many years running away from any thoughts of family, and now I want to run headlong toward it. Because you and Savannah have given me the one thing that was missing from my life."

His voice cracked, so I squeezed his hands. Tears were flowing down my cheeks, and Gabe reached up to gently swipe them away.

"What I'm trying to say is that you've made me happier than I ever thought I could be. Charlotte, you and Savannah have made me whole. And that's why I have to do this."

He took a half step backward, then lowered himself to one knee. I choked out a sob as he reached into his pocket.

"Charlotte Rhodes, will you spend the rest of your life with me? With *us*? Will you marry me?"

It didn't feel real—all my dreams coming true. I shut my eyes and shook my head, overcome by shock and surprise. When I looked down at Gabe, his face was a mask of worry. "Yes!" I laughed as his expression transformed into relief. "Did you have any doubt? A million times yes!"

I threw myself at him, and he fell to the ground with me on top of him. I kissed him hard on the mouth, despite the tears flowing down my cheeks.

"Are those happy tears?" he asked in between kisses, sounding bewildered.

"The happiest," I laugh-cried. "Because you're home, with us, forever."

"That's exactly right," he agreed. "We're all home for good."

END OF SEAL'S SURPRISE DAUGHTER

Do you love sexy SEALs? Please keep reading for preview from my next book, *Valiant* and *SEAL's Ward.*

THANK YOU!

Thank you for choosing my book.
If you're keen to read more heart-pumping, fast-paced romances by me, then please help me, by leaving an honest review.

Want sexy military men straight to your inbox? Then sign up to my mailing list at:
www.leslienorthbooks.com/katie-knight

ABOUT KATIE

It isn't a big surprise Katie Knight ended up writing romances about the stellar, studdly men of the Navy SEALs; after all, she was a K-9 trainer for the SEALs and met her own Navy SEAL hero husband while preparing one of their K-9 partners for combat. A few years after their marriage, her and hubby decided to retire with their K-9 partner, Sam, to raise their children in the Midwest. It wasn't long after that before Katie decided to write her own stories featuring the men of the SEAL teams and the women who love them.

When not imagining dangerously romantic scenarios for her heroes and their feisty heroines, Katie enjoys hikes with her husband and Sam, spending time with her children, and long runs (on and off the beach).

To learn more about Katie you can check out all her books on social media and her website: www.leslienorthbooks.com/katie-knight

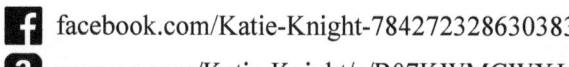

facebook.com/Katie-Knight-784272328630383

amazon.com/Katie-Knight/e/B07KWMCWXJ

ABOUT LESLIE

Leslie North is the USA Today Bestselling pen name for a critically-acclaimed author of women's contemporary romance and fiction. The anonymity gives her the perfect opportunity to paint with her full artistic palette, especially in the romance and erotic fantasy genres.

Find your next Leslie North book visit LeslieNorthBooks.com or choose:

BY TROPE

BY HERO

PS: Want sneak peeks, giveaways, ARC offers, fun extras and plenty of pictures of bad boys? Join my Facebook group, Leslie's Lovelies!

BLURB

For a Navy SEAL, love is a dangerous game…

Navy SEAL Christopher Williams was fine with the idea of staying out of his ex-girlfriend and son's life. After all, that seemed to be what Kelsey wanted, and he never planned on becoming a father. But when it becomes clear that Kelsey and their baby are in danger, Christopher doesn't hesitate to charge back into their lives—at least for a little while. But as they spend time together, the gruff SEAL begins to wonder if he should finally make the situation permanent….

Kelsey may have mixed emotions about Christopher, but there's no denying she feels better now that he's here to protect her and their son. Her Navy SEAL father has gone missing, and it seems like someone wants to use her and her son as bait to force his return. She knows Christopher won't allow her to be hurt or captured…but her heart is in danger as well. The longer Christopher stays with them, the harder it is to resist falling back in love with the sexy SEAL.

With time slipping away and the bad guys closing in, Kelsey realizes everything she holds dear is in peril—including her newfound feelings for Christopher…

Grab your copy of *Valiant*
Available April 14, 2022
(Available for pre-order Now!)
www.LeslieNorthBooks.com

EXCERPT

Chapter One

It wasn't like he'd been expecting a joyful reunion with Kelsey Reeves given their rocky past, but the expression on her face was still a shock. Mouth downturned, eyes hard. She stared at him through the cracked front door like she didn't trust him.

Given what he was about to tell her, that had to change. Immediately.

"Well?" She crossed her arms protectively over her chest.

Cole realized with a start that he'd been staring at her. It wasn't like he could help it. Angry or not, Kelsey was still the most beautiful woman he'd ever seen. Porcelain skin, hair that changed with her moods. A smile that made everyone want to smile back at her.

Not like he'd be seeing *that* any time soon.

But he could understand why her walls were up. Their breakup had left them both wounded even though he'd been the one to end things.

"I came to talk about your dad," he said, and her dark hazel eyes instantly flared to life. "Can I come in? I don't want to get into it on your front porch, if you know what I mean."

"Have you heard from him? Is he okay?" Her arms dropped along with her defensive posture, and she leaned toward Cole. "I've appealed to the Navy for information, but they've been no help. They keep stonewalling me."

"We need to talk inside," he repeated. "Somewhere where we can't be overheard." He'd parked down the street and watched her house for several minutes before approaching. He hadn't seen anything to worry him, but he didn't like to be exposed standing outside her door.

"Oh, I guess." She stepped back through the door, holding it open so he could enter. With one last scan of the street, Cole stepped inside the small foyer. Once the door was shut, he threw the deadbolt behind him. Kelsey raised an eyebrow but didn't comment. The extra lock wasn't a great deterrent, but it was better than nothing. He blinked and looked around as his eyes adjusted to the dimmer light. From what he could see, her house hadn't changed much, except for a diaper bag sitting on the floor near the door.

His son was here.

The thought of the baby, *his* baby, somewhere in the house left Cole feeling off-balance. He pushed the feelings down. He'd made a choice

—even if it was one that he doubted every day. He'd have to shoulder the consequences.

Kelsey led Cole down the hall and as they passed the family room he could see a dark-haired woman he didn't know kneeling in front of the sofa, blocking his view of the babbling infant. He paused briefly, hoping that the woman would shift, and he'd get a glimpse of his child.

"This way," Kelsey said as she shot him a look over her shoulder. It was clear that she didn't want him anywhere near Eddy.

It's not like he could blame her.

She wheeled around once she walked into the small kitchen. "What do you know? Tell me my father is all right."

Cole wished he could say that and bring her some comfort, but the situation involving Lieutenant Commander Edwin Reeves wasn't looking good. The Navy had officially listed her father as AWOL and viewed his disappearance a month ago as both voluntary and suspicious. No one had heard from him since...until that morning.

"I'm not sure how he is," Cole said, "but I got an email from him today."

"Oh my God, I've been so worried about him." Kelsey clutched her hand over her heart and dropped her head so that the mass of her pink ombre hair obscured her face. She sniffled then cleared her throat and composed herself. "So he's alive and well enough to get a message to you. What did he say?"

Cole held back for a minute, knowing that what he had to tell her wasn't what she wanted to hear. Edwin was under a shadow of suspicion for his unsanctioned disappearance—and the suspicious timing. Cole wasn't buying any of it, since he'd trained under and fought beside the man and knew he was no traitor. Edwin was the straightest arrow Cole had ever known, but the situation looked damning.

"Cole, talk to me," Kelsey demanded, her tone sharpening at his silence.

"The email was scheduled, so I can't speak to how he is currently." He hesitated and then went on. He wasn't really supposed to share this information with civilians, but she deserved to have some details that might explain her father's actions. "Kelsey, about a week before your dad went AWOL, a SEAL team was ambushed—it seems that the attackers were tipped off by someone who knew where they'd be. The team was almost wiped out."

"Almost?" Her fair skin paled.

"Only two survivors." The loss of so many good men had rippled through the ranks. The SEALs worked in teams, but the teams weren't isolated from each other. They often shared training and even missions. Cole had personally known four of the men who lost their lives, and knew of others. "They're both in critical condition still and are unable to tell what happened."

"I'm so sorry to hear that, but what does it have to do with my dad?" He watched her frown and knew that even as she asked the question, she was already starting to piece the intel together in her head. She understood the military as only a kid who'd grown up in it could, and she possessed a sharp, analytical brain from her work as a software coder.

"The ambush has been linked to a leak in military intelligence," he said. "It's believed that someone high up, someone who would know where that team was, sold the coordinates."

She slumped back against the wall, her hand going to her mouth in shock as she realized what he meant. "Dad would never...never...you know that."

"I do, but not everyone is seeing it that way." Cole would stake his own life on Edwin's loyalty to the Navy and his country. But that wasn't enough to clear his name. "The timing of his disappearance may be unrelated, but it's calling his integrity into question."

"After all the years he's dedicated to the Navy, how could anyone think that of him?" She straightened as her anger returned, but it wasn't directed at Cole this time. "What exactly did the email from him say? I want it word for word."

Cole pulled out his phone and opened his email, knowing that she wouldn't be satisfied with his recitation of the short message. "See for yourself." He handed her the phone.

"If you receive this," Kelsey read aloud, "the situation is worse than I feared. I need you to keep Kelsey and Eddy safe until I send word that the threat has been neutralized." She looked up at him. "What threat? Why does he think we're in danger?"

"I don't know, but I plan to do as commanded," he answered. Edwin must have had reason to believe his daughter and grandson were vulnerable. Cole wished he knew what the specific danger was, but the message hadn't contained any details. Didn't matter. The email was tantamount to an order in Cole's mind, even though it meant he'd been tasked with protecting the woman he'd dated and cared for and their four-month-old son, whom he'd never even met and hadn't expected to. He'd removed himself from Kelsey's life when she told him she was pregnant with his baby because that's what she seemed to want from him. She'd flat-out stated that the baby would be better off with just a mother who would always be there versus also having a father who was gone for long stretches like hers had been. He'd agreed, for mostly the same reasons. She thought he couldn't offer the kind of commitment she wanted, and she was right. That wasn't because he was in the military, though.

It just wasn't in him. He wasn't built that way.

He and Kelsey had ended their relationship that December night, but it hadn't kept Cole from thinking about her and the baby. They were constantly in his thoughts, and he'd been grateful when she'd notified him in July that their son had been born healthy. Cole had been overseas at the time, which he viewed as a good thing. If he'd been in California, he might not have been able to keep his distance. Twice he'd allowed himself to look at pictures of Eddy that Kelsey posted on her Facebook page. But he didn't want to make a habit of that. He'd made his choice, one that seemed in the child's and Kelsey's best interests, and he had to live with that.

But things were more complicated now that he'd been called on to ensure their safety. It was a hell of a position to be in.

"There's something I'd better show you," Kelsey said.

"The baby?" The question was out before he could stop it. Instantly, he regretted it. If he wasn't going to be in the boy's life, it would be easier not to have any contact with him.

Kelsey cast a glance over her shoulder toward the family room. "That's not what I meant. Wait here—I'll go get it."

Cole tried not to stare after her as she walked out of the kitchen, but it was almost impossible for him to ignore her curves.

She came back a few minutes later and held an envelope out towards him, a stoic expression on her face. "I found this in my mailbox yesterday. I think you should read it."

He took the envelope, noting that there were no markings on it, and pulled out the single page. The typewritten message was brief and harsh. *Locate your father by the end of the month or you and your son will suffer the consequences.*

No signature. He turned the paper over, looking for clues to who might have sent it, but there was nothing, not even a postmark. It had clearly been hand-delivered. He re-read the message, his concern flaring into something deeper. It was already the twentieth of November, giving them just ten days to comply with the demand.

But that wasn't what made his blood burn hot in his veins. The threat did that. Cole had seen enough horror in the world during his three years as a SEAL to grasp what those consequences might look like for a woman and baby. No way was any of that happening to Kelsey and their son. Edwin had entrusted him with preventing that—and more than that, Cole himself was now fully committed to their safety.

"I have no idea where to look for Dad," Kelsey said, sounding remarkably calm for a woman under such a threat. She had to be frightened, but she was tough and refused to show it.

"Why didn't you contact me as soon as you got this?" he asked, but her only reply was a tiny shrug, reminding him that they'd made the choice for her to be on her own with the baby, and that was what she'd planned to stick to despite the dire situation. "I will protect you, both of you." He wanted her to know that. He'd do whatever it took, which started with finding out as much intel as he could about Edwin's disappearance.

"I guess Dad suspected that things could go wrong with whatever he's doing, or he wouldn't have scheduled that email for you. I just wish I knew…" She trailed off and glanced out the window, her fear seeping through her calm façade.

Cole wanted to pull her into his arms in the worst way, to reassure her that everything was going to be okay. He could almost feel her pressed against him, the sensation of her body seared into his memories. But he knew that if he did that, he'd be reminded of everything he'd walked away from. And hell, it wasn't likely that Kelsey even wanted his touch. Not anymore.

"We'll figure it out and find him." His hand grazed hers as he gave the letter back. He could give her that promise at least, and his pledge to keep them safe. Kelsey's eyes met his, a current passing between them. He couldn't decide if he wanted to rub the feeling away or hold onto it. Either way, being back this close to Kelsey was dangerous.

Grab your copy of *Valiant*
Available April 14, 2022
(Available for pre-order Now!)
www.LeslieNorthBooks.com

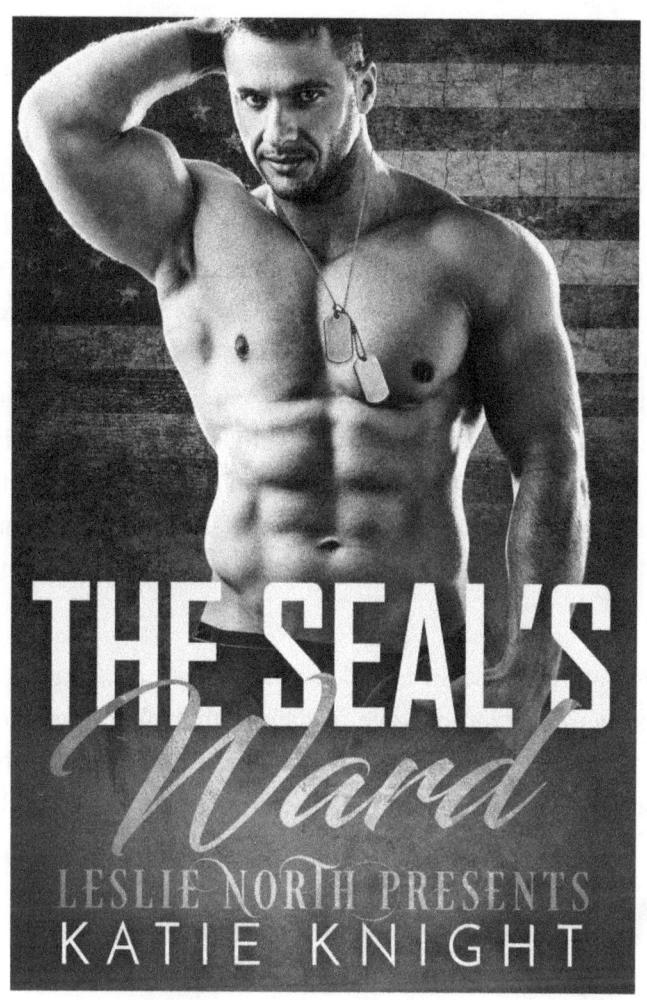

BLURB

Former Navy SEAL Jed Tremayne knows discipline, hard work, and how to carry a rifle. So when his two best friends die suddenly and leave their daughter, Nala, in his care, Jed's a little out of his element. Though he wants desperately to connect with her, Nala has withdrawn further and further into her books. Jed just needs a little help, and decides to hire a nanny, and who better than someone who loves to read as much as Nala does? Sure, Tess Frederick is a bit too intriguing, a little too sexy in an adorably unconscious way, but she instantly connects with Nala so Jeb gives her the job.

Tess likes things ordered. But lately, her well-planned life has descended into a bit of chaos. Haunted by the suicide death of her former lover, and recovering from her bookstore going out of business, an open position for a private tutor seems like the perfect job to take while she figures out the rest of her life. Nala is an adorable and intelligent little girl and the two have an instant connection. Her guardian, Jed, is another matter altogether. Too good-looking. Too intense. And too sexy by far. If Tess can just get through the next few weeks with her heart intact, all will be well. The thing with hearts, though, no matter how hard she tries, she can't seem to turn hers off.

But as Jed and Tess begin to fall for each other, an unknown danger threatens their burgeoning love, a danger that blindsides them both and threatens their very lives—and the life of the little girl they both love. Can two broken souls find the strength to conquer this dark menace or will they be lost in the fight to survive?

Grab your copy of *The SEAL's Ward*
www.LeslieNorthBooks.com

EXCERPT

Chapter One

"I'm sorry. Could you repeat that, please?"

Jed Tremayne, retired Navy SEAL and current private security for hire, had faced down enemy snipers and charged directly in the line of fire to defend life, liberty, and honor. Yet, at this moment, he'd never felt more incompetent in his life—all because of the eleven-year-old girl currently sitting at his kitchen table with her nose stuck in a book, as usual.

The snooty administrator from the private school gave an aggrieved sigh. "I'm sorry, sir, but your daughter is just not making adequate progress in her classes, nor does she socialize with the other children. She is not assimilating into the student body sufficiently to meet her needs or ours."

Nose wrinkled, Jed held his phone away from his ear and scowled down at it, taking a calming breath before responding. "First of all, she's not my daughter." He flinched slightly at the words. The girl glanced over at him before returning to her story. Cursing under his breath, Jed walked from the kitchen into a little alcove near the pantry for privacy. "I mean, she is my daughter, sort of. She's my ward and she lives with me." He left unsaid that their living situation was because Nala's parents were killed in a car accident not long ago. Surely, the administrator already knew—and he didn't want to say it aloud so that Nala might overhear. Her parents' deaths had hit her incredibly hard. She didn't need additional reminders. "All of this should be in your files." He exhaled slow and scrubbed a hand over his close-cropped brown hair. "Listen, we're both doing the best we can here. Can't you give us a break?"

Asking for help wasn't a skill Jed excelled at. It wasn't in his nature. He'd been raised to prize independence, to trust only himself, to live by a strict moral compass and remain in control at all times. All things that had made him a huge success as a Navy SEAL.

All things that were causing him to be an enormous failure in the parenting department.

None of this was a surprise—even the phone call he was currently enduring. In truth, he'd realized that he needed help about two weeks after Nala had come to live with him. Between the crazy hours and danger associated with his security jobs, and Nala's issues with socializing and adjusting to her new life, their road to resettlement had been bumpy, to say the least. Their mutual grief over the loss of her parents only made things worse.

Nala's father, Martin Jackson, had been a member of Jed's SEAL team. They'd been good friends. Hell, Jed had even served as best man at Martin's wedding to Nala's mother, Ayesha. He'd known Ayesha too, both of them having grown up in the same rough neighborhood here in Baltimore. He'd been the one to introduce Martin to her. The three of them had been tight. When the call had come in six months ago about the car accident that had killed them, he'd been devastated. Even more so when he'd gone to collect Nala from her home and bring her here. Neither Martin nor Ayesha had any other family to speak of, and they'd chosen Jed as Nala's godfather, never imagining he'd be called on to step into the role of parent.

It all seemed like a horrible dream, except the reality of this nightmare was all too real.

He shook off the past and did his best to focus on what the administrator was droning on about now. "…follow my suggestion, it would work out best for all of us."

"I'm sorry." Jed rubbed his hand over his face. "I didn't catch that."

He could imagine the administrator's pinched expression and sour frown at the other end of the line. Like that old *Saturday Night Live* sketch of the Church Lady, but on steroids. "I said that we believe it's in everyone's best interests to remove Nala from classes at the present time. We would suggest hiring a private tutor for her until such time as her social anxiety issues can be dealt with properly."

Perfect. Jed managed to resist his impulse to slam his fist through the nearest wall in frustration and instead gripped his phone tighter. The plastic case cracked under the pressure. "Homeschooling? Seriously? Don't you think she'd do better being around other kids right now instead of isolating her at home? How is she supposed to hone her social skills with no one to talk to?"

"She can talk with you and with her instructor, Mr. Tremayne," the administrator said with a derisive sniff. "And please don't raise your voice to me. I'm trying to help you with this situation."

Then why does it feel like another kick in the teeth?

Jed swallowed those words and inhaled deep to slow his pounding pulse. With his background, he'd dealt with plenty of people like her —thinking they were so much better than him, thinking they were above it all in life, above all the petty problems and dirty deeds everyone else in the world had to deal with. Still, he'd hoped things would work out for Nala at the school. It had one of the best ratings in Maryland for helping kids with special needs. Apparently, those needs didn't extend to stutters. Or bereavement. Or being one of the few black kids in an otherwise all white school.

Dammit. Jed let his head fall back, and he stared at the ceiling. It wasn't like he hadn't tried to find help for Nala. Lord knew he'd been interviewing nannies since the day after she'd moved into his restored Victorian house. Many had applied for the job, none—so far, at least —had passed muster. Too old, too young, too judgmental, too lax. It was getting to the point he feared there wasn't a person alive who could help him or Nala.

Even the therapist had tried to assist with the search, sending over several people for him to talk with about the job. But there'd been no good match. All he wanted was someone kind and caring and truly concerned about the little girl who'd lost so much already, someone who connected with Nala in a way that no one so far had, not even Jed.

He'd tried, God knew he had. Making her dinners, watching movies on Netflix, even buying her a special, limited-edition *Harry Potter* series box set because he remembered Martin telling him one time it was her favorite. So far, all his efforts had netted him was a greater understanding of Moana than any thirty-six-year-old man should have, and Nala withdrawing even more because she constantly walked around with her nose stuck in a *Potter* book.

There was one interview left today and if this one didn't work out, Jed wasn't sure what he was going to do. He'd talked to a new potential client a few days prior and if things worked out, it could mean he'd have steady hours and income for the foreseeable future. But only if he had the situation with Nala squared away.

"Mr. Tremayne? Are you still there?" the administrator asked. "Hello?"

"Yes. I'm still here," he said, his flat tone betraying none of the tension roiling inside him. Marvelous. So now he needed not only a nanny, he needed a tutor capable of homeschooling his kid. Jed leaned back slightly to view Nala, still sitting at the table reading. She looked so small and vulnerable it made his chest ache. All alone in the world and so, so young. His battered heart yearned to make things better for her, and he said a silent prayer for help doing just that. She reminded him of himself as a young boy in so many ways. Granted, his parents were still alive, though he'd not talked to them since the day he'd left to join the Navy. They might as well have been dead for all he cared. For all they'd made him suffer growing up.

Whatever happened, he refused to put Nala through the same tortures he'd faced simply for being different from what others expected. The snooty administrator and her snooty school could both go hang. He and Nala would find their way together, no matter what it took. Jed saw this as a new mission, a new op, and he would not, could not, fail at this. "Fine. Consider Nala no longer a student at Rucks Academy. I'll find a suitable tutor and homeschool her until we find a better facility for her needs. Your academy is woefully inadequate for a special girl like my Nala. Perhaps you should take a good look at your own values and prejudices before inflicting them on an innocent child. You don't deserve her as a student, and you could do with a bit more diversity and inclusion at Rucks."

"Sir, I hope you're not implying—"

"I'm not implying anything. Goodbye." He ended the call abruptly.

Feeling an odd mix of vindication and apprehension, Jed slowly walked back into the kitchen.

Nala didn't look up at him as she spoke softly. "W-was t-that Ms. B-borchelt?"

Jed grabbed a pale ale out of the fridge and twisted off the cap. He wasn't usually much of a drinker, especially this early in the afternoon, but he needed something to take the edge off, and one ale would hardly do him any harm. At six-two and two-hundred pounds, he could've drunk a whole case with minimal side effects. Another skill from the SEALs—he could hold his liquor.

After a few long swallows, he set the bottle aside on the counter and leaned his hips back against the edge of the granite. "How would you feel about taking your classes here for a while?"

She shrugged and turned a page in her book.

"I'll hire a tutor, someone you like, and they can teach you right here at home," Jed continued, used to one-sided conversations lately. "Maybe someone who likes to read the same books you do. I've got a new lady coming for an interview today, in fact. A friend of mine recommended her."

He glanced at the clock. His latest interviewee should be here any time.

"I-I d-don't c-care," Nala stammered, a slight frown creasing her brow. "She w-won't l-like me anyw-way."

The sound of the doorbell cut through the kitchen like a knife and Jed sighed. He wanted to counter Nala's pessimism with some optimism, but the truth was that his luck with finding a nanny had not been good. He had no reason to suspect his odds of finding a suitable tutor would be any better.

"I'll just get that," he said, picking up his bottle and taking another swig as he strode out of the kitchen and down the hall to the front door. His friend at Walter Reed who'd recommended Tessa Frederick to him had described the woman as smart, efficient, and conscientious —all traits Jed would need to see demonstrated for himself before even considering hiring the woman. She had apparently worked as a speech therapist and once owned a bookstore, which he guessed were decent qualifications, though he'd prefer someone with more direct child care experience. He'd reserve judgment until he'd seen her for himself.

Forcing a smile he didn't feel, he yanked open the door to find the exact opposite of what he expected. The female standing on his stoop looked flustered and rumpled and far younger than he'd expected. Wind whistled around her as she brushed a few strands of honey blonde hair from her eyes and flashed him a tentative grin. "Uh, hello. Tess Frederick. I'm here to interview for the nanny position."

Jed battled an unexpected intrigue over her slight lisp and her hesitant expression and stepped aside to allow her entry. He didn't miss the way her gaze dropped to the bottle in his hand and he resisted the urge to tuck the bottle behind his back. He was not going to defend drinking a beer. He cocked his head to the side. "Right. Please come in."

Grab your copy of *The SEAL's Ward*

www.ingramcontent.com/pod-product-compliance
Lightning Source LLC
LaVergne TN
LVHW041242060125
800614LV00004B/793